The Very Thought of You

S. Anne Gardner

Affinity
eBook Press
NZ

Table of Contents

The Very Thought of You

© S. Anne Gardmer 2003

Affinity E-Book Press NZ LTD
Canterbury, New Zealand

ISBN: 978-0-9922461-9-8

This is a work of fiction. Names, characters, places, and
incidents are the product of the author's imagination or
used fictitiously and any resemblance to actual persons,
living or dead, businesses, companies, events, or locales is
entirely coincidental

Editor: Ruth Stanley
Cover Design: Helen Hayes

Acknowledgements

Thank you to my lovely partner who asked for this story and it is because of her that it was written. Lisa, you have been such a gift to my life in so many ways I could not possibly count. Thank you, for loving me, for believing in me in the darkest of times and for sharing with me the best of times. You and the children that we have shared keep my heart and because of all of you, my loves, I am breathing. Here is your love story; I wrote it for you.

To my sons, I am grateful for all the memories and all the love; you have always been the softness inside me. Each one of you have been the miracles in my life.

To my friends who have listened and listened…thank you.

Thank you to Mel and Julie who have believed in this book and have published it.

Dedication

For Lisa, who asked me to write her a love story.

Chapter 1

She didn't know exactly when it happened, but she suddenly realized that she had lost something important. Something inside her had died. She looked out the window of her corner office at Bakeman, Thomas and Denton. She had made partner and was what many would call a success. As she looked out that window, she asked herself why she was there. There was a snowstorm passing by, a nor'easter no less. All others had left for home but she was still there, working. And, at that moment that morning, she realized she had lost something. She had lost it so slowly that she didn't even know when it started or when it ended.

She had lost the joy she once had at just waking up and looking into the eyes of her only child. It had been two years since Teddy had died, two years since she had barely seen anything. If she were honest with herself, she would acknowledge that that was the exact moment it had happened, but to do that would mean she would have to look at it. And even now, Teddy was not something she could talk about with anyone.

Her marriage to James, Teddy's father, from the beginning had been shaky at best, and she couldn't be sure at that point why she had ever married him. In the beginning, she thought it was because she and James had the same interests and a shared love of the law. But as the years had gone by, she realized that her marriage was just a lifeless entity that served no purpose. She had decided to discuss divorce proceedings with James when she discovered she was pregnant.

And, for a while, Teddy caused them to try to make it work. But in the end, they both realized that they would make better parents if they were apart. It had been just another weekend for her when the phone rang. James always called before dropping Teddy off on Sunday afternoons, so she picked up the phone expecting to hear James's voice. But, that day, when the phone rang, it was not James but the police. She couldn't remember exactly what they said or what happened afterward; it was all a blur of pain and more pain that never seemed to end. All she could process were the details—the cold and antiseptic details; all else simply disappeared from her mind. Perhaps it was a blessing or perhaps it was all a part of the nightmare of the nothing that she felt day in and day out.

They had both died instantly. Hit head on by a drunk driver. Her life became a list of things that had to be done, no feeling, a persistent numbness that seeped in like freezing rain; a coldness that steals all the warmth inside you. She never, ever again felt warm after that. The cold had taken over inside her, like a frozen tundra. People were so kind, they took over decisions like what clothes her son should wear; the flowers, the church, even the plot where Teddy and James should be buried. They began to pack up his room and at that she simply began to scream and yell, demanding that they all leave her house. It was her son, his room, and it was up to her to do what she wanted with it. They had called her a few times to ask how she was doing, always avoiding the mention of what had happened. Relatives and friends called; Kate, her sister, had tried to talk to her over and over again but she simply just didn't want to talk. All she wanted was the one thing no one could give her; she wanted her son. After a few weeks, they all went back to their lives, she didn't. After a while, she went back to work. Work was what had kept her sane. She worked and she worked. Work was a stream of life-lessness that was filled with words, contracts, and other people. Work was where she lived and where she functioned. She had never done better profes-sionally; work had become her life.

Two years later, she was looking out of her big office window seemingly in full control of her life. *Her life. Is this what it is going to be like for the du-ration?* She had become used to the routine. She got up in the morning, went to the office, and didn't leave until after nine each night taking work home with her. On the weekends she would work some more.

She had slowly separated herself from her friends and family. It had happened so slowly that they had stopped trying to include her. And that was fine with her because not feeling was so much bet-ter. Work was something that she had control of and understood. She ran her fingers through her hair not understanding why all of a sudden these things filled her mind, much like the nor'easter that was hitting the area with such force.

She was brought out of her thoughts by the ringing of the telephone. "Hello."

"Alex, how did I know you would be there?" asked the voice on the other end of the line.

"A good guess, Elliot. What do you want?" she asked sarcastically.

"Alex, the weather is getting really bad out there. Although I can't fault you for your dedication, I don't want to see you stuck in the building all weekend." He said it jokingly but the concern managed to slip in.

Elliot Harford was a senior partner at the law firm and also a friend. He had known Alex when she had been married to James and had seen the changes take place in her after the death of her ex-husband and her son. In effect, he knew more about her than most, so he knew she would be in the office. Elliot had always liked Alex and James but he, like many others, thought that sooner or later she and James would divorce. It was that obvious to anyone who knew them. He had to admire her for trying to make the marriage work for Teddy's sake.

And, he had been there by her side when she buried her ex-husband and son. Little by little the old Alex that he liked disappeared and he missed her. She was effective, efficient and one of the best lawyers, if not the best, in his law firm. However, the woman that she had been had changed. What made her sharp and lethal in the courtroom was a different person than who she had been once upon a time. There had been a softness about her that had simply just disappeared. And he missed that part of his colleague and his friend.

"There are some things I need to go over with you before we go to trial on the Eldrige case. I wanted to check out a few facts..."

Elliot cut her off. "Alex, it looks like Siberia out there. Go home!" His concern was obvious in his voice.

"I'm almost finished here, Elliot," she stated in a matter-of-fact tone.

"Okay, be careful driving home, Alex. See you on Monday."

"Yes, sure, I'll see you Monday, Elliot," she replied absently as she hung up the phone and went back to her brief.

†

An hour later, she got into her car and started home. It had snowed more than she had expected and she maneuvered her Mercedes slowly down the street. There were only a few cars on the road as most people realized it was not worth taking a chance driving in such horrible weather conditions.

As she came close to an intersection, a car suddenly pulled out in front of her and spun out of control. She swerved to miss hitting the car. The other car, however, did not manage to keep control and slammed into a snowbank to the right of the road. Alex pulled over and took a deep breath to regain control of her shaking body from what just happened. She looked up at her rearview mirror and could see the driver of the other car; the driver's head was leaning on the wheel. Alex picked up her cell phone and dialed 911 but there was no signal whatsoever. She tried once more then just acted on instinct; Alex opened her car door and ran back toward the other car as quickly as she could through the heavy winds of the raging snowstorm.

When she reached the other car, she knocked on the window. She could see a woman with blonde hair with her head resting on the steering wheel. She tried opening the door but it was locked. Alex looked around the interior of the car and was able to make out the crying of a child coming from the backseat. Alex tried the door again then the door that led to the backseat from the driver's side; both were locked. She could see a little girl in a car seat in the back and the persistent crying began to scare her. She tried banging on the glass again to see if the driver might hear her. And when the blonde's head moved, she felt a rush of relief.

She knocked on the window again, signaling the woman to unlock the door. The woman leaned over and pulled up the lock before she fell back on the seat. Alex pulled the door open and could see a gash on the blonde's forehead, which was bleeding profusely. As she looked at the blonde woman's face, the beauty of the woman before her struck her. It seemed odd to her that she would notice that under the circumstances. She shook her head as if to come back to reality and then looked at the little girl who was quietly sobbing and had begun to hiccup as tears ran down her face. She pulled up the lock to the back door, then closed the driver's side door gently to protect the woman inside from the wind still coming in strong gusts around them. She opened the back door to tend to the child who seemed somewhat calmer as she reached out slowly for her.

"Okay, it's going to be okay," she said gently to the little girl who bravely tried to control her sobbing.

"Mommy...is mommy okay?" she finished saying as another sob escaped her.

Alex looked to the front and then back at the child. She could tell the child the truth that she didn't know anything about the woman's condition, which is what her sterile mind assessed. But, looking into those blue, tear-filled eyes, she did the only thing she could think of, she lied.

"She is going to be fine. We are going to get you both into my car and get you to the hospital," she said confidently to the child.

"My arm is hurt. Mommy was taking me to the hospital, I fell off the counter," she said. "I wanted a cookie and I fell." She started sobbing again.

"Okay, okay...it's okay, what's your name?" Alex smiled, trying to soothe the little girl.

"Carly..." the little girl replied as she sniffled and wiped her runny nose with her arm.

"I like it..." was all that Alex said and the little girl giggled and smiled.

"Okay, Carly, I am going to get you out of your seat and into my car and then I will get your mom, okay?" Alex waited patiently and finally the little girl nodded her head in agreement. She unbuckled the child and bundled her up in a blanket that she noticed on the other side of the seat before starting back to her car with the little girl in her arms.

Alex finally reached her car and could not help but shake as she strapped the little girl into the backseat; the cold was going right through the lightweight coat she was wearing. She was about to start back for the woman when she felt a small hand hold on to hers.

"I'm scared," the little girl said.

Alex reached out and put a golden curl back behind the child's ear. "Everything is going to be fine, angel." The child stared into her eyes and Alex was touched by the look of trust she saw there. "I'm

going to get your mommy. I'll be right back, okay?"
Carly nodded.

Alex braved the cold again as she began to make her way back to the other car. When she finally reached the other vehicle she opened the driver's side door. The woman inside turned her head slowly to her, her eyes still closed. She looked at the pale face of the beautiful woman before she reached in and tried to unbuckle the seat belt. As she removed it, the woman's eyes fluttered open.

When blue eyes met green ones, the world suddenly stood still. It felt like fusion, or when suddenly all stops and nothing else filters. All Alex could hear was her breathing and all she could see were those blue eyes. And as the lips of the woman opened slowly, Alex's eyes focused on the lips, mesmerized by them. A strong gust of wind shook the car and Alex out of her trance.

"Can you move?" she asked softly.

"I think so..." The woman suddenly got very agitated. "Carly!"

"Your daughter is safe in my car; she's fine, a little shaken up but otherwise fine," Alex said reassuringly.

"My head," the woman complained before her head fell back again to the seat.

"You probably have a concussion. I'm going to try and get you into my car and then we can try getting to the hospital," Alex said, making an effort to sound calmer than she actually felt.

The blonde shook her head in affirmation.

"Okay, come on. I'll help you out and you can lean on me, okay?" Slowly Alex helped the injured woman out of the car. As the woman stood upright, she fell forward into Alex's arms clinging to her as her head rested on Alex's chest.

"Slowly...a step at a time." They began walking toward Alex's car fighting against the gusts of wind and snow. Once they reached Alex's car she helped her into the front passenger's seat and strapped the seat belt on as gently as she could so as not to cause any further pain. As she did this, her passenger seemed to lose consciousness. Alex closed the car door and ran to the other side and got into the driver's seat.

"Is my mommy going to be okay?" asked the little girl bravely.

"Yes, sweetheart. We're going to the hospital now." Alex looked at the woman next to her, and then focused on the road as she headed for the nearest hospital.

†

Alex sat in the sterile waiting room of the hospital, waiting. The last time Alex had been in a hospital was when James and Teddy had died and the police had taken her to identify the bodies. She just sat quietly, lost in a time she had never truly left behind. It was a familiar scene that she didn't want to remember, but one she couldn't forget. Those were the details that she could not erase from her mind: the smell of antiseptic, the whiteness of the walls, and the colors that they all wore, white, sterile white. All the details were so embedded in her psyche that she could not remove them. There were no feelings, no emotions just a cold bluntness to it all. And Alex found herself back to the dark time in her life. When she was taken to see them, she remembered thinking that Teddy looked like he was just sleeping. How could he be dead? He had been such a beautiful boy. As all those memories washed over her yet again, the pain was still a constant but the tears still never appeared.

Suddenly two little feet stood on a piece of the floor that she had been staring at. Alex's eyes came up and before her stood Carly with a cast on her little arm.

"Hi," she said to Alex.

Another voice spoke to her. "I'm Doctor McKensey."

Alex looked up and saw a young man dressed in a white coat.

"She will be fine. It was a simple break. Her mother has a concussion and we would like to keep her overnight for observation." As he spoke to her he began writing on a pad.

Carly slipped her small hand into Alex's, and she looked down at the child who was leaning against her.

"Here is a prescription for some Tylenol with codeine in case she is in a lot of pain. Some children are okay taking it others get really fuzzy. Her mother needs to take her to her pediatrician in a week to check the cast." The doctor nodded and handed her a piece of paper.

"Doctor...McKensey, was it?" The doctor nodded. "Her mother..."

"You can go in to see her in a minute, she is a little disoriented. You can pick her up tomorrow if all is well. I don't, however, see any complications at this time," he was saying as a nurse approached him.

"Doctor McKensey, we have a double gunshot wound coming in through emergency."

"Doctor...wait...I can't..." Alex tried to say but the doctor rushed off as the sound of a siren filled the emergency area.

Carly squeezed her hand and Alex looked down at her. "I told them you brought me and mommy in and you would take care of me," the child said.

Alex's mouth dropped open and then closed again. She knelt down so she could speak at the child's eye level. "Carly, won't your daddy be worried?" Alex gently asked.

"I don't have a daddy."

"Well, isn't there anyone that will be worried if you don't go back home?"

"No, it's just me and mommy."

Alex ran her fingers through her hair not knowing exactly what to do. Perhaps the mother could answer some of these questions. She didn't feel well. Her head felt crowded with cobwebs and memories that always left her in a state of confusion and disorientation. She would ask the mother. *The mother would know who to call.* She felt a pulling on her hand and Alex looked down at the child.

"What's your name?" the little girl asked.

"Alex...my name is Alex," she said, looking into sleepy baby blue eyes. "Come on, sleepyhead; let's go see your mommy."

Alex pushed the door to the hospital room open and slowly walked toward the woman lying on the bed.

"Mommy!" Carly ran toward the bed as Alex brought a chair over next to the bed for the child to stand on and see her mother.

"Mommy," the child said again, touching her mother's cheek.

The woman's eyes fluttered open and a smile slowly filled her face. "Baby, are you okay?" she whispered.

"I'm okay, Mommy. Alex is taking care of me."

"Alex," the mother murmured as her eyes closed again.

Chapter 2

With the confusion at the hospital and the memories swirling inside of her, Alex found herself just taking the child home with her. It was not a choice made with logic or the lack of it, it was simply one made by a child who put her hand in hers and trusted that she would be there. And Alex needed to make sure that this little girl would be taken care of.

She took Carly home with her and together they walked to Teddy's room where Alex tucked a sleepy Carly into Teddy's old bed. It felt surreal in a way; but it also made her feel that it was so right. She had tucked in a child and it filled her with emotions she thought she had forgotten and with emotions she thought she could and would never feel again. She closed the door slowly and walked into her bedroom. There was a child under her roof again and a stranger with blue eyes that filled her thoughts.

As Alex got ready for bed she pondered the evening's events. The emergency room had been busy that night; there were car accidents, people arriving by ambulances with heart attacks, and gunshot wounds. She wondered how the doctors and nurses did it day in and day out. How could they work with such horror each and every day?

It was no surprise that they just assumed she would take care of Carly. But her legal mind also told her that they had left themselves open to a giant lawsuit. For that matter, so had she. Her mind was not working rationally she kept telling herself. Something had happened tonight; no…something had been happening to her for a long time. Her personal life had been in limbo for a very long time now. Tonight was the first time in a long, long while that she had acted on pure emotion. It made no sense for her to have brought this child home with her, but she had. All she knew was that when Carly had put her little hand in hers emotions overwhelmed her. She needed to think, this she realized, but she was so confused that logic obviously had had no place in her decision-making this night.

Alex decided to just stop thinking; overthinking was one of her biggest problems. She would deal with it all in the morning. She was tired. And there were the blonde woman's blue eyes that somehow had not left her thoughts. Maybe she knew the woman from somewhere. Perhaps they shopped at the same stores or even met at a business dinner or something. Alex lay down in her bed not able to take another step or think another thought. She knew she had acted irrationally tonight. So many things were flooding her mind. Alex was sure she knew Carly's mother from somewhere.

And of course, there was the fact that this woman's child was sleeping in Teddy's room. Alex took a deep breath; and as usual she expected the anxiety to begin and to go through another sleepless night. But, instead she was filled with an unexpected sense of peace.

There is a child sleeping in Teddy's room. With that thought, she closed her eyes and slept through the night for the first time in two years.

†

"Alex, I'm hungry," said a small, soft voice.

Alex opened one eye and then the other and sat up in bed with a startled surprise as she stared at a little girl with golden curls who was standing next to her bed. She rubbed her eyes and looked at the child again, and suddenly the events of the night before flooded her mind.

"Are we going to go see mommy?" the child asked softly.

"Um...well, let's see. Let's have some breakfast and then we can go to the hospital and see your mommy," Alex said with a smile. "Okay?"

"Do you think she missed me last night?" Carly asked as her lower lip quivered.

"Carly, I am sure that your mommy is going to be happy to see you. If we hurry and have our breakfast maybe we can get there before she has hers. We can pass by the gift shop and get her a present. Would you like that?"

The reasoning seemed to pacify the child and a bright smile filled her face with the thought of surprising her mother with a present.

Alex got out of bed and went to her closet. She chose a pair of jeans and a designer T-shirt. She hadn't worn jeans in such a long time. They never seemed appropriate since all she had done for the past two years was work. She remembered the last time she had worn jeans she'd gone to see Teddy play little league.

A small voice interrupted her thoughts.

"Alex, do you have kids?"

Alex froze on the spot. She felt the space of the closet closing in around her as her breathing became somewhat ragged. She could only hear a strange buzzing in her ears, and she realized that she was experiencing the beginnings of a panic attack. Her knees felt week and she could feel the nausea and fear building. The panic that usually followed began.

"Alex?" A little hand took hold of her hand and pulled her out of the closet.

"Sit down, Alex, you don't look so good," Carly said as she walked her to the bed. "I'll get you some water okay? Wait here."

Alex tried to concentrate on her breathing. She closed her eyes and remembered the doctor's instructions. It had been so long since she'd had an attack. She rubbed her leg to focus and then tried to see herself in a quiet place.

"Here, Alex, drink this," Carly said as she guided the glass to Alex's mouth. "You are probably tired. My mommy had a very bad cold once and she got really tired. I remember I got her a glass of water and she felt better."

Alex opened her eyes and drank the water as instructed.

"Feeling better now?"

Touched by the concern she saw in the child's eyes Alex, without thinking, caressed the soft cheek, and kissed the child's forehead. "Yes, Carly, I feel much better. Thank you." She slowly began to breathe easier.

Alex's reward: a lovely smile. She caressed the child's hair. "You are very sweet, Carly."

"Mommy calls me her sweet pea."

"I feel much better now. Let's get ready and go see your mommy."

†

An hour later, woman and child walked into the hospital. Alex kept going from one scenario to another in her head. How the hell was she going to explain that she had taken a child home and brought her back the next day? Had she lost her mind? No, she wasn't going to go there; what she had done had been completely insane.

With anticipation, Alex walked a little faster as she got closer to the door of the hospital room where Carly's mother would be waiting. She wanted to get it over and done with. As soon as she opened the door, she was faced with a hysterical woman and several very anxious hospital personnel.

"Where is my daughter? Oh God, where is my daughter!"

"Ms. Owens, please calm down. We have notified the police and they are on their way," a very anxious nurse was saying.

"Mommy!" yelled Carly as she ran to her mother. Immediately her mother's head turned and her arms opened, welcoming her child into her embrace. The nurse closest to the hysterical mother picked the child up and helped her onto the bed.

"Baby! Oh, God...baby, are you okay?" Reese Owens asked as she held her child tightly against her. She kept asking the child the same thing over and over again as tears of joy ran down her face.

All eyes turned to Alex.

A dark-haired nurse spoke first. "You took the child without her mother's permission!" she said accusingly. "The police have been called and are on their way so you better not be going anywhere."

"Well, I'm glad they are on the way because this child was handed over to me last night by a Dr. McKensy and an emergency room nurse. They let me take her home without asking so much as a single question. They didn't even ask who I was. So yes, please have the police come. I think there should definitely be some charges made as to the ineptitude of this hospital. I would say that the hospital is definitely liable for this." Alex was furious as she continued. "You people have no excuse for what happened here last night. Someone could have hurt that child!" a very indignant Alex yelled, pointing to Carly. Then she pointed at the hospital staff. "Get out! I want to speak to Ms. Owens alone." Alex was angry, but she also realized that she had acted just as irresponsibly. Right now all she could think about was that if it had not been for her someone else might have hurt Carly.

They all stood speechless, shocked by the enormity of the accusations.

"*Now!*" she yelled.

Everyone walked out quickly. Alex then turned her attention to Reese Owens and was met again by those blue eyes. Alex's stance relaxed and she walked over to the woman in the bed. As she got closer, she put her hand out. "Hello, I'm Alexandra Masters."

"I don't know whether to thank you or kill you," said the very angry blonde. She took Alex's hand and as the connection occurred, their eyes fused, both women felt a sudden jolt as the connection was made. Blue eyes searched green ones. "If you have hurt..."

"Alex took good care of me, Mommy." Reese's attention went back to her daughter and she released Alex's hand.

"I'm sorry you were worried," said Alex softly.

Reese's eyes went back to Alex.

"Alex made me eggs just the way you make them for breakfast, Mommy," said Carly as Reese's eyes went from one to the other.

"I'm really sorry you were worried. Last night it seemed the only thing to do. We came in here to speak to you and you kind of passed out," Alex said with a kind of floppy smile as she tilted her head.

Reese looked at the woman before her unable to believe her incredible attraction to this stranger amidst her anger and worry for her daughter. "Did you bring us to the hospital?"

"Yes."

"Thank you. I'm not quite sure what happened," she said as she looked back at her daughter. "I'm so glad to see you, sweet pea." She touched the cast. "Does it hurt very much?"

"No...um...only a little. Mommy, Alex has a little boy and I slept in his room last night. He has that castle I wanted from the toy catalog. Remember, Mommy? Maybe Alex can tell us where she got it," said an excited Carly.

Reese looked up to see a very pale Alex. For one instant, before the curtain of cold came down, she saw so much pain in those green eyes.

Alex's face turned to Carly and a soft smile appeared briefly on her face before she turned her attention to Carly's mother. "Here is my card, Ms. Owens, I'm sorry that I cannot stay. If you have any questions please contact me and I will be more than happy to answer them. I was glad to be able to help you and your little girl." Once Reese took her business card, Alex walked toward the door.

"Wait!" called Reese, and Alex froze as she was about to open the door. "I…I think we got off on the wrong foot."

Alex turned to face her. "You were in a car accident last night. I brought you and your daughter to the hospital. I was, by great negligence, given your child to take home, I would sue these people if I were you. I took your child home with me and then I brought her back safe and sound to you today. I have a deposition to work on. I don't think there is much else to discuss. Have a nice day, Ms. Owens." Alex then stopped, took a deep breath, then spoke again much softer. "I regret that you were frightened…I'm sorry, I only wanted to help and perhaps I acted badly…" Alex looked up and met Reese's eyes. "I'm sorry I scared you..." She exited the room leaving a very confused Reese behind.

"Did I say something wrong, Mommy?"

Reese looked down at her daughter. "No, honey. Miss Masters just had to go to work," she said, reassuring her daughter before looking down at the card Alex had given her.

†

Alex almost ran down the hallway. When she reached the outside of the building, she leaned against the wall of the hospital and attempted to regulate her breathing. The cold air kept hitting her face. She focused on the solidness of the concrete she was leaning against. She felt dizzy and the shaking began to take hold of her body. She kept telling herself that it was going to be okay. When she began to feel more in control of her breathing it began to get a little easier. *Control.* She kept saying over and over again to herself. When she began to acknowledge her surroundings she slowly walked back to her car and drove home. Alex felt confused and scared; the panic attacks were back.

When she got home, she went directly into Teddy's room and cried. She had not cried since that day when they told her Teddy was dead. Alex had simply turned something off and not allowed herself to feel the pain. But, as she looked around her son's room, she finally allowed herself to feel the loss of him. She fell to her knees. Seeing Carly in Reese's arms reminded her of what it had been like to hold Teddy. Oh God, she remembered how it felt to hold and love Teddy. And finally, after two years, she allowed herself the tears. And when the tears finally came she couldn't make them stop. Alex didn't work for the remainder of the weekend. She didn't do much of anything, hardly leaving Teddy's room. She had finally faced losing her child. And as she accepted his loss, she found the pain unbearable.

Chapter 3

Alex went into the office on Monday a week later and, as usual, buried herself once again in paperwork.

Elliot noticed the slight darkness under her eyes but said nothing that morning. Alex had not missed a day of work in the last two years and when she let them know that she was taking a week off no one questioned her. Alex tried very hard to go on as if nothing had happened, but something had and Elliot knew that eventually she would come to him and discuss it. They had been friends for years, although in the last two he, as well as others, had felt severed from Alex's life. He, though, still held onto hope that one day she would come back. After another week had gone by and Alex had not approached him, he decided to just go into her office and plain ask her what had happened.

"Alex, you have a minute?" Elliot asked as he poked his head into her office. Alex looked up from the paperwork on her desk.

"Sure, Elliot, come on in. I have to ask you a few questions in reference to—"

"Alex, what's wrong?" He cut her off before she continued.

"Wrong?" she inquired as she looked back up at Elliot again.

"Yes, what is wrong?" He took his time in saying the words, waiting for some kind of response from her.

"I don't know what you are talking about," she answered, looking back down at her paperwork. "Elliot, in reference to this case…"

"Alex, I can tell there is something wrong," he insisted.

"Elliot, just let it go, okay." The buzzing of her intercom interrupted the conversation. Alex pushed down the button and spoke. "Yes, Carol?"

"Ms. Masters, there is a Ms. Owens here and she insists she must see you," said a harried Carol.

Alex said nothing for a moment. Elliot noticed her hesitation.

"Ms. Masters?" asked Carol again.

Alex shook her head as if shaking out of a trance. "Give me a minute, Carol, and then please send her in." She quickly released the button and took a deep breath. Reese Owens was in her office.

"Alex?"

Her eyes looked up and were met with a very curious look on Elliot's face.

"Elliot, I met this woman and..."

"Alex, do you want me to…"

Before Elliot could finish his sentence, the door to the office opened and in walked Reese Owens.

Blue eyes met green ones and again that feeling of déjà vu hit Alex. Both women became once again lost in each other's eyes.

Alex stood up slowly behind her desk.

Elliot coughed.

Alex snapped out of it first and looked at Elliot. "Elliot, will you please excuse us?"

"Alex, are you sure?"

"Elliot, I will address your concerns at another time," she said, dismissing him.

Reese was surprised by the change in the other woman's demeanor. Alex's eyes had seemed soft but quite suddenly she had become very cold.

"All right, Alex," Elliot replied just as curtly and walked out of the office.

†

Alex's eyes went back to a curious Reese. "Won't you sit down, Ms. Owens." She pointed to the chair in front of her desk.

"Yes, thank you," Reese said as she sat.

"What can I do for you?" Alex asked as impersonally as possible as she sat down behind her desk.

"I wanted to thank you for what you did for me and Carly. She told me how kind you were to her." Reese leaned forward in her chair. She gave Alex a brilliant smile. "She hasn't stopped talking about how Alex did this and Alex did that. And she is right, you were very kind and I am very grateful. I called but your secretary told me that you were out for the week so…"

Alex just looked at the woman in front of her, mesmerized by the voice.

Reese looked down as she blushed. "I know I wasn't very nice to you in the hospital that day. I guess...I'm not used to kindness for kindness' sake." She looked up again.

Alex was struck by the vulnerability in the woman's eyes, and she found it difficult not to be moved. She found herself wondering what had happened to this beautiful woman to make those eyes become so guarded and fearful. Alex said nothing as she continued to stare at the woman.

"I wanted to come before today but..." Reese trailed off.

Alex was staring, saying nothing.

"Look, I'm sorry to have bothered you. I just wanted to thank you." A visibly upset Reese got up and started walking toward the door.

"Wait!"

Reese turned around and came face-to-face with Alex, who had rushed out from behind her desk to reach her.

"Please, don't go," said Alex. "Please?" She reached out and touched Reese's arm.

Both women stood at arm's length, staring at each other.

"Alex, I just wanted to thank you. I can see that you are a very busy person," Reese said nervously and held her hand out in a gesture of goodbye as she took a step back.

Alex took it and again they both felt the jolt.

"Would you like to have lunch with me?" asked Alex without breaking contact.

"Yes, yes, I would."

†

Reese walked into her house and as she was hanging up her coat smiled to herself thinking about the time she had just spent having lunch with Alex. It had been so long since she had met someone she liked. Alex was such a paradox. But a mystery, that for some reason, she thought was worth taking a chance on. The woman was incredibly distant one minute and then her eyes would tell another story. Yes, Alexandra Masters was indeed an interesting puzzle to solve.

Reese walked into her living room and sat down, folding her legs under her as she sat on her sofa.

"Who are you, Alexandra Masters? And why do I feel such a connection to you?" Reese asked aloud. "There is so much strength in you and yet...there is so much sadness. What happened to you, Alex?"

Reese was lost in her daydreams when she was brought back to reality by the ringing of her telephone.

†

Lunch had been wonderful. Alex went back to the office after dropping Reese off at home since her car was still in the shop for repairs. She had enjoyed herself. It had been so long since she had just gone out to lunch simply just to be with someone.

Reese and the way they connected fascinated her. They had talked for hours. Reese had asked her no personal questions, almost as if she knew not to ask any. Instead, they talked about the things they enjoyed and the books and the movies they both liked. Alex slowly relaxed and eased into the experience. She found something in those gentle eyes that when they looked at her they touched something inside her so deeply that she could not explain. A smile gradually appeared on her face and stayed.

She sat behind her desk for the rest of the day and somehow managed not to get any work done.

†

For two days, Alex kept telling herself the only reason she could not get Reese out of her mind was that it had been such a traumatic meeting. On the third day, she picked up the phone and dialed.

"Hi, Reese. This is Alexandra Masters," she finally managed to say when Reese answered.

"Alex, hi!"

"I remember you telling me that you were going to be free this weekend and well...there is this movie I wanted to see and I figured that maybe..."

"Yes, I would love to, Alex!" a very enthusiastic Reese answered.

"Oh, great!" Alex finally breathed normally.

"Hey, how about if we meet here for dinner before the movie?" asked Reese.

"Sure, that sounds great. I'll see you Saturday then."

"Till Saturday, Alex."

"Oh, Reese?"

"Yes?

"What time? Dinner I mean?" Alex finally asked and they both began laughing.

†

By the time Saturday arrived, Alex was a nervous wreck. She had tried on numerous blouses and slacks. She found some fault with each one. Finally, she sat down on her bed in exasperation.

"What am I doing?" she asked herself out loud. "I am acting like a teenager on her first date. She is just a woman I met. Under bizarre circumstances granted…but, it doesn't merit this." She shook her head in confusion.

After giving herself the speech about how little this all meant to her at least half a dozen times she started going through her closet yet again. Finally, she settled on a pair of navy blue slacks and a cream V-neck sweater. She checked her hair and her makeup at least five times more than usual, picked up her coat, car keys, and purse, and walked out her door a mere two hours later.

†

Reese had been running around all day as well, telling herself to just keep it simple. It was just going to be dinner and then going to see a movie she reasoned. Carly had gone to stay with a friend for a sleepover so she didn't have to worry about when they would get back from the movies. Alex arrived at Reese's house promptly at five. She pulled her black cashmere coat closer to her, fighting the cold wind as she walked up to the front door. She hesitated for a moment then knocked waiting only a second before the door swung open.

Reese's face filled with a huge bright smile as she pulled Alex in by her arm. "Hurry in here, you silly goose. You look like you're half frozen already," she said to Alex playfully.

"Yes, I am half frozen," Alex answered soberly, shaking from the cold.

"Here, give me your coat and let's go sit near the fire." She helped Alex off with her coat and pointed to the fireplace. Alex walked slowly toward the roaring fire; she looked around the room and found it pleasing. She liked the soothing cream colors and the plush, overstuffed furniture. It was a lovely room she told herself; somehow it was just like Reese.

The warmth from the fire was comforting. She found herself mesmerized by the flames. Her attention focused on them, she took in a deep breath and relaxed. It occurred to her, at that moment, that by just standing in front of the fire that she felt a sense of peace that she had lost so long ago. What she felt at that moment was very simple. She felt good. So lost in her thoughts, she didn't hear Reese come into the room. Reese's house felt like a home. She remembered that she once had that and in one instant, it was all gone.

†

Reese quietly sat down to the side of where Alex was standing and just looked at her. Alex was so beautiful. Her first memories of the woman were hazy and brief. She recalled her at the car, in the hospital for a very short time, and the morning when Alex brought Carly back to her. In some ways, all the visions she had of Alex were different, and yet, somehow they all made up who Alex was. If she had to describe Alex, it would be aloof, controlled, and confident…but there was more, so much more, she had also had a brief look at the insecure and lonely woman that day during their lunch together.

Reese sat lost in watching Alex—very much like the flames had captivated Alex. Reese had been enthralled to the point of speechlessness with Alex's beauty, then with her spirit, and finally with the woman who guarded herself against the world. Her lunch with Alex a week earlier had been very informative. Alex was a private person and she carried a great pain. Reese remembered the look of it every time she spoke of family or of Carly. Alex spoke of nothing personal. Reese picked up the cues and, after a while, she said nothing personal either. Her reward, the woman opened up. After that, the time just flew and she was allowed to see a curious, bright, sensitive woman who was lonely. And now, here was Alex in her living room, lost in her thoughts. At least this way she could look at her and admire her beauty without worrying about being caught staring.

Reese had been attracted to her from the very first moment. However, she was not sure if Alex felt the same way. There were looks exchanged and nuances; sometimes such things could be misinterpreted. Yet, she hoped. She had never felt such a strong attraction to anyone. She had been alone for so long, thinking only of Carly.

Meeting Alex brought back all the things she missed, but hadn't realized she missed until they met. Alex was so beautiful just standing there. All she had thought about since the woman's call was the Alex during lunch, the Alex who rescued her, the Alex who had been so loving with Carly, the Alex who was so vulnerable. Alex, Alex, Alex.

God, she thought she would die if she didn't kiss Alex. Almost as if her thoughts had been expressed aloud Alex turned and stared at her.

"I'm sorry. I guess I just got lost in the fire," she said, smiling at Reese dreamily.

"Here," Reese patted the sofa, "come and sit down."

"This is a lovely room. It's warm and welcoming," Alex said as she looked around.

"Thank you. Can I get you something to drink?"

"Oh, sure…that would be nice. A Diet Coke if you have one."

"Okay, coming up," Reese said as she left the room.

Alex sat back and allowed her head to lie back, hoping to rest for a moment. It had been such a long time since she had just relaxed. She remembered thinking *I am just going to put my head back for a minute* and as she closed her eyes, she drifted into sleep.

Reese walked back into the room and stopped in front of the sleeping woman. She put the soft drink on the coffee table and went back into the kitchen to check on dinner. She returned to the room several times and found Alex resting so peacefully that she didn't have the heart to wake her. Reese guessed it probably had been a long time since Alex was able to just sleep like that.

Dinnertime came and went as Alex slept. Reese put another log on the fire, sat down next to Alex on the sofa, and decided to read a book. As the time passed, her eyes also became heavy and sleep overtook her as well.

†

The sound of whimpers woke Reese. Reese looked at Alex who appeared to be having a nightmare. Alex then began sobbing. "No...no…please no…" Alex kept repeating.

Reese moved closer and caressed her face hoping to soothe her. Reese could not help but notice how soft Alex's skin was to her touch.

45

"Alex, wake up, it's only a dream," she said softly into Alex's ear.

Alex seemed not to hear and progressively became more agitated.

Reese shook her a little bit, as she got even closer to her. "Alex, wake up." Reese repeated a bit louder than before.

Alex's eyes fluttered open. She had a look of such grief in her eyes and as soon as their eyes met Alex's filled with tears that just overflowed. Reese took her into her embrace and held her tightly as Alex began to sob even harder.

"It was only a dream, sweetheart. You're safe. It was only a dream," murmured Reese into Alex's ear softly. She didn't know how long she held her until her sobs began to slow then stop. She kept reassuring Alex as she stroked her hair. After a while, she realized that Alex was breathing normally again.

†

Alex lifted her head slowly wondering about the connection she had with Reese. She had cried

46

her eyes out in front of a virtual stranger when even her family had been unable to comfort her. And yet, Reese made her feel comfortable and confident. She gave into the sense of familiarity. When Alex's eyes searched Reese's eyes, they were completely vulnerable and open. She hid nothing of herself.

Reese was struck with the openness of Alex's eyes and in return, her eyes said so much that it seemed natural to lean forward and kiss Alex's lips.

Alex had seen her leaning in slowly and was unable to break the connection as Reese's lips met hers. Warmth spread all over her body. Her eyes closed as she leaned into the kiss, her lips opened, welcoming Reese further into the kiss.

Soft lips asked and the plea was answered and the kiss progressively became more demanding. What began as a soft kiss became passion-filled, with a hunger and longing that neither woman had planned or expected.

A moan escaped Reese's throat as her hands began to pull Alex closer to her.

Alex reached for Reese also and then quite suddenly she pushed her away as the horror of what they had just shared hit her. She stood up to put distance between her and Reese, almost tripping over her own two feet as she was backing away.

"Alex, wait…" Reese said, her hand reaching out to Alex.

"No, I don't want this. I…I'm sorry, but I don't want this," Alex said, her eyes darting all over the room in desperation. "Where is my coat…I have to go."

"Alex, wait, please don't rush off like this. We can talk about this," begged Reese as she got up and walked toward her.

"Look, there is nothing to discuss. I don't want this. You should not have kissed me!" she said in a louder voice.

"I don't remember you pushing me away," answered Reese sarcastically.

"You got me here under false pretenses!" accused Alex.

"You forget; you are the one that called me, Alex!"

"Where is my coat, damn it!"

Reese went to the closet, took out the coat, walked over and handed it to Alex trying to control her temper. "Here, run away, Alex."

"Listen, I am not running from anything, I am not that way, okay!" she exclaimed, reacting in anger at what Reese was implying.

"You certainly were giving me all the right signals!" Reese shot right back at her.

"I was not!" Alex exclaimed in indignation.

"You invited me to lunch, you invited me to the movies, you accepted my dinner invitation…and Alex, you kissed me back!" Reese told her as she counted with her fingers, staring at Alex for an answer.

Alex remained silent, took her coat and put it on with quick, jerking motions. As she was about to walk out the door she looked briefly at Reese, she opened and closed her mouth as if to say something then she simply turned and left, slamming the door behind her.

✝

How could this have happened? kept repeating in Alex's head.

"No way!" She started talking to herself out loud as she paced her living room floor. "I never encouraged her. People have lunch all the time. Jesus! They go out to the movies and they don't end up..." She paced some more. "But...they don't end up kissing." She stopped pacing and just stared out the window. She shook her head incredulously. What had she done? How had she gotten herself into something like this?

She walked over to the telephone hesitated only for an instant and then picked it up. She dialed and waited for the person on the other side to pick up.

"Hello?"

"Katherine?" She spoke softly.

"Alexandra, is that you?"

"Yes, it's me. How are you?" Her voice sounded strained even to herself.

"Alexandra, what's wrong?"

"Kate, I need to see you..." she said barely above a whisper.

"Alex, I'm on my way."

The line went dead and Alex hung up the telephone. She sat down in her dark living room and waited for her sister.

Chapter 4

"Well, Alex, you should be flattered!" said Elliot.

"Thank you, Elliot."

"That was some compliment Peter gave you at dinner last night."

"Which one?" She laughed.

"Yeah, very funny. I have to admit I never thought you would pull it off," he said to her.

Alex looked at him quite seriously. A bit peeved, she asked. "You doubted my ability?"

"Never your ability, Alex. I just never thought you were the jugular type." He faced her, getting ready for what was to come.

"I go into trial to win, Elliot. That's my job. I'm sorry if my winning this case disappointed you," she finished sarcastically.

"What the hell is happening with you, Alex?"

"What the fuck are you talking about, Elliot? Why is it that you are forever acting like my father?"

"I guess I miss the old Alex," he said softly.

"Well, she's gone…so get over it."

"Don't you care about anything or anyone anymore? What has gotten into you? Yes, you won that case, Alex, but you were ruthless. That old man didn't need to be humiliated by all those things you brought out in court yesterday. I am not only talking to you as your friend but as one of the partners in this firm."

"I won, Elliot," she stated plainly.

"Yes, you won Alex. How do you feel?" he said and then walked out of her office.

†

Alex looked at the closed door and realized that Elliot had never given up on the old Alex. The old Alex…she couldn't even remember her anymore. The past…why should she want to remember the past? What did it hold for her but pain? And somehow, it also brought her to when Carly had been in Teddy's room, and of course that brought her to Reese. Memories then flooded her of Reese by the firelight, Reese in the sunlight, Reese in the snow, and always Reese in her arms. And Reese's mouth…

Carol's voice came over the intercom. "Ms. Masters, your sister is on line four. Do you wish to take the call?"

"Yes, thank you, Carol, I'll take it." Alex was grateful for the interruption.

†

Reese had hoped that once Alex had a chance to think things over she would call. She never did. At first, she was mad, then the anger became sadness because Reese knew she had seen something special happening between them.

Alex just didn't care enough. Somehow, no one ever cared enough. She had been dealing with being second-best her whole life. And yes, for a while she indulged in self-pity. How could she have been so stupid to fall for someone that quickly?

As the months went by, she convinced herself that it had all been a mistake. If Alex refused to acknowledge what she had felt that was her problem. She wished she could move on. But, somehow, even after all these months, she would occasionally remember and long for that moment and that kiss.

"Alex…" she said, savoring the moment until her daughter interrupted.

"Mommy, come on we are going to be late!" Carly said as she tugged at her mother.

"Oh, sorry, sweetheart. Yeah, let's go. Did you grab your glove?"

"I got it. Can we go to McDonald's after the game?"

"Yeah, I think that sounds great." She grabbed the small bag next to the door, and they both walked out to the car to drive to Carly's little league game.

†

"Katherine, I'm busy, I can't go to a baseball game!"

"Alexandra, you promised him. It's going to begin at four thirty this afternoon. Alex, he's gotten to know you again and he loves you. And, Alex, I think you need this too," she finished softly.

"Kate, I will make it up to him."

"Alexandra, be there!"

The line went dead. And Alex stared at the phone in disbelief.

"She sounds mad," Alex said as she hung up the telephone. "I hate baseball."

Her intercom buzzed again and Carol spoke. "Ms. Masters, your sister on two."

"Thank you, Carol." She switched extensions. "Yes, Kate?"

"By the way, Kevin asked me to remind you that you promised to take him to McDonald's after the game."

"Okay, okay! I'll be there. I might just be a little late, but I will be there."

"Bye."

"Bye, Kate."

Her sister Katherine was sometimes a tyrant, but Kate had always been there for her. After Teddy died, not even Kate could reach her. And then, after that night with Reese… *God! Always Reese.* "Why can't I get this woman out of my mind?" she asked herself. She would finish the brief tomorrow and go see Kevin's little league game. Alex closed the file she had been working on and for the first time in a long time she allowed her mind to run free. She had made some changes in her life—some was better than none she told herself. Alex knew that change was necessary; she also admitted to herself that she was not sure where the changes would take her.

She had taken a more active part in her sister's and nephew's lives since the night she had called Kate after her incident with Reese. That's how she thought of it these days. She kept telling herself that she had been caught in that situation because she was lonely. So Kate, good old reliable Kate, had come through for her again. And she had to admit she enjoyed spending time with Kevin, her nephew.

Spending time with her family was Alex's way of justifying the rest of her life. She was a true paradox. She had gotten softer she told herself and yet she had never been harder than she was now. Elliot was right; she had become ruthless and it was beginning to show.

†

"Come on Carly, throw it!" yelled Reese.

The team was practicing before the game began. Carly was a member of the Blue Jays. She loved to play but, unfortunately, she was not very coordinated. Reese patiently tried to teach her to throw the ball over and over again.

"Okay," she replied, throwing the ball to the right side of Reese.

Reese ran to catch it. It had rained the night before so the practice field was somewhat muddy and in some places there were patches of mud. As Reese caught the ball, she slid in the mud. All she remembered was hitting something really hard and landing on her bottom. She sat up and looked down at herself covered in mud. Looking to her side, she came face-to-face with what she had run into.

Next to her in the mud sat a furious Alex, wearing a gray business suit. The white blouse, skirt, and jacket were covered in mud, as were her legs, hands, and even some parts of her hair.

"What do you think you were doing!" Alex yelled at a somewhat shocked-looking Reese.

"I was trying to catch…I'm sorry, Alex."

"Dear, God, this mud is cold!"

Reese got up, wiped her hands on her pants, and extended a hand to Alex.

"Here let me help you up."

"No! Just stay away from me!" she yelled, trying to get up but she kept slipping in the mud and landing on her bottom. "Shit!"

"No...mud," said Reese, who began to laugh.

"This is not funny, Reese!"

"It is from here. Now are you going to let me help you or not?" she asked sweetly.

"No! I can get up myself." Alex almost made it up before her foot got stuck in the mud. Her shoe would not let go of the mud and she fell on her stomach this time.

"Okay, enough, here let me help you," Reese said, and as she was helping Alex up, they both landed back on their bottoms.

This time they both looked at each other and started laughing. Some of the parents and most of the kids had become spectators of the mud party. When they heard all the laughter, they both looked over at the crowd they had attracted. Kate was one of them.

"Okay, shall we try this again?" asked a laughing Alex.

"I'm ready if you are," said Reese. They helped each other stand and walk away from the sea of mud they had been in.

Kate walked over with Carly and Kevin behind her. "Well, you two are a sight."

"No mud jokes, okay, Kate," Alex said with a smirk.

Kate put her hands up. "And land in the mud with you? Oh no!" She too started laughing.

"Hi, Alex!" exclaimed Carly with glee as soon as she saw her.

"Hello, sweetheart, how is that arm?" she asked the little girl.

"Good as new. See?" She showed Alex her arm and moved it around and bent her wrist.

"Yep, it looks good to me too," she agreed, laughing.

"Mommy, you are really muddy!" Carly laughed, wrinkling her nose.

"Yes, honey, I really am." Reese looked at herself up and down and began to laugh as well.

Kate just stood there with a big grin on her face. She was about to open her mouth when Alex gave her the famous look of death and her mouth shut again.

"Kate, this is Reese Owens," Alex said to her sister, avoiding eye contact. She knew that it wouldn't take Kate long to figure things out.

Kate turned to Alex and instantly put two and two together. Alex had never told her the last name of the Reese she had referred to that night, but she knew exactly who it was by the way Alex was acting. She then chose to run with it and see how things would go. For now, she would play the game that Alex was obviously not able to own up to. "I know Reese, Alex. Kevin and Carly are on the same team," Kate said simply.

"Kate is your sister?" Reese asked incredulously.

"Small world, huh?" answered Alex, knowing full well by the way Kate looked at her that she knew that this was the Reese they had discussed.

"Yes... Hi, Kate," said Reese before turning back to Alex.

"Why don't you two go get cleaned up. I'll watch the kids till you get back, and we can all go to McDonald's afterward. You can go to my house it's closer. Alex, you know where my sweats are. Hurry up you two, the game is about to begin." As she said this, she walked off with Carly and Kevin in tow. "Come on guys, the game is about to start."

Alex had been silent and Reese had looked nervous at the suggestion so Kate knew she was on to something. Since losing Teddy Alex had run from her emotions. Seeing Alex nervous and unsure now was all Kate needed to know that it was a very good thing for Alex to deal with whatever her feelings were about Reese. Alex had told her about that night with Reese, but what Alex did not know was how much more Kate had seen in the few minutes she had just witnessed; more than Alex had intended, definitely. Alex had always been fearless. Even from childhood she had this light that she brought into everything and everyone. Alex had just simply forgotten or denied anything that might touch her since she had lost Teddy. Kate knew Reese and she liked what she saw. *If only Alex would bother to look, she might be surprised.* She knew Reese to be an incredible person, and she only hoped that Alex would allow herself to live life again.

"Um, well…no sense in taking two cars," said Alex. "We can go in my car." She looked at Reese.

Reese looked at her for a moment. "Okay, your car then. Lead the way, old muddy one." They both started laughing as they walked toward Alex's car.

†

Once they were both in the car, they were engulfed by the silence. Alex just looked at the steering wheel and Reese kept staring at her hands, neither one saying anything.

"Reese...I'm sorry..."

"Alex, it's okay," Reese said, looking at Alex now.

"I…"

"Alex, this is where we meet okay? A new start…" She looked at Alex, holding her breath.

"Friends then?" Alex asked tentatively.

"I would like that," said Reese with a big smile.

"Good, I missed you." Alex started the engine and looked back at her rear window.

Reese just smiled.

†

Reese and Alex began seeing each other again. There were occasional stolen glances and light touches, but it never progressed past that. They began rebuilding from the disastrous beginning of when they met. Slowly, each woman became a part of the other's life. They planned weekends together with Carly. Occasionally, Alex would stop by after work and then gradually she started staying for dinner. And before she knew it, the only thing they were not doing together was sleeping under the same roof.

So much had changed in those few months. And yet, some things seemed not to at all. One afternoon, the inevitable happened…

"I want to go to McDonald's," said Carly.

"Carly, we cannot live in McDonald's," said Reese as Alex walked through the door.

"Hi, small fry," said Alex.

"Alex!" Carly ran into Alex's waiting arms.

Reese just smiled.

"Hey, that smells good," said Alex as she walked closer to Reese with Carly in her arms.

"Cookies."

"Hey, small fry, you're getting heavy. Have you grown since yesterday?" she asked jokingly.

"No," Carly answered with a giggle.

"Alex, let's go to McDonald's," Carly pleaded.

"You're early," said Reese looking at Alex.

"Yeah, I figured it was a beautiful day so I'm playing hooky."

"Great, you hungry?" asked Reese as she kept spooning cookie dough on the flat cookie sheet.

"McDonald's, please?" whined Carly.

"I have an idea. Why don't we have a barbecue and jump in the pool over at my house." Alex looked at Carly and began tickling her tummy.

"Can we Mommy? Can we please?"

"Sure, that sounds great. Let me finish the cookies and I'll get our suits."

"Maybe we can rent some videos too, if you want, for later," Alex said, looking at Carly. Reese had gotten used to the way Alex had adopted asking them to spend time with her.

"Okay, maybe I should follow you in my car so that you don't have to drive us back later."

"Hey, it's Friday, and I have plenty of room. Why don't you guys just stay over?"

"Oh, Mommy, can we? Can we, Mommy?" Both Alex and Carly were waiting for her to answer.

"Okay, I know when I'm outnumbered," she said, then wiped her hands clean, put the cookies in the oven, and went to tickle Carly.

†

"Is it ready yet?" asked Carly.

"Almost, sweetheart. Do you want to help Mommy bring out something for us to drink?"

"K," the little girl said as she ran inside.

Alex smiled. *She is such a sweet little thing, beautiful just like her mother.* That thought had slipped out innocently enough. Alex thought about it. *Yes, Reese was beautiful, with her golden hair and the bluest eyes that could look right into your soul. And her mouth...Reese's mouth is soft and inviting.* She mentally shook her head. *It is happening again,* Alex thought. She was thinking about Reese in that way again. At that moment, Reese walked out of the house wearing a cobalt blue bathing suit and Alex could only stare.

"Come on, Carly, so I can close the door, honey," Reese said, oblivious to the hungry look on Alex's face.

"Okay, Mommy."

"Put those cups on the table, okay." Reese looked toward Alex. She was both surprised and pleased by the look on her friend's face.

"You like it?" she asked as she turned to show off her suit.

"Yeah, it looks nice." Alex looked quickly down at the barbecue.

Reese smiled with renewed hope. She had caught Alex looking at her. So many times she had found herself looking at Alex, imagining what it would be like to kiss her again. So many times Alex had touched her and just as quickly changed the subject or just walked away. Reese had wondered if she had imagined it all. But not today. She recognized the look she had seen on Alex's face because she knew what wanting was.

Reese had tried so hard not to think of Alex in that way. Having Alex as a friend was better than not having Alex at all. After a while, she came to realize that she treasured the friendship they had built. And although Reese was happy to see desire in Alex's face, it frightened her since Alex had not been able to handle her feelings before.

It had hurt when Alex ran away that night. It had hurt a lot. But now, she didn't know if she could endure the separation. Reese had to face, at that moment, that she had fallen in love with Alex She wasn't sure when it had happened exactly but at that very second she knew it to be true; she was in love with Alex. The enormity of it all hit her suddenly, and at that moment Reese realized that she would rather have Alex as a friend in her life than not have Alex in her life at all. Love with Alex scared her; Alex had run before and might run again if Reese were to change the dynamics of their relationship.

Carly walked over to Alex again. "Are they ready yet?"

"Yep, they are ready." She gave the little girl a big smile.

"Yeaaaa," Carly said, hopping up and down.

"Let's eat," said a triumphant Alex.

They sat down, ate, and were amused by Carly's antics. Both women soon forgot the awkwardness of the previous moment as they laughed at Carly, and when they finished eating they started playing in the pool.

†

"Throw it, Carly!" Reese kept yelling. They were playing monkey in the middle and Alex was in the middle. "Come on, honey, throw it!" Reese yelled again, laughing at Alex who was slowly walking toward the giggling child. She then threw the ball and Reese caught it in midair.

Alex turned and played the same game, walking slowly toward Reese with a wicked smile on her face. Every time she was about to throw it, Alex would get in the way.

"Run, Mommy, run!" Carly screamed in glee.

Reese turned and attempted to run in the water.

Alex caught up with her and pulled her against her body. "I've got you," she said into Reese's ear.

Suddenly, the heat between them exploded and their bodies melded together. Reese could hear Alex's breathing close to her ear and felt Alex's arms tighten around her stomach, pulling her tighter against her. Suddenly, Carly appeared in front of them.

"You lose, Mommy, Alex caught you," she said, laughing.

"Yes, honey, Alex caught me." Reese was surprised that Alex was still holding her tightly. She turned in Alex's arms. Blue eyes met passion-filled green ones. She thought Alex was about to lean down and kiss her when Alex released her from the embrace.

"I'm going to catch you, small fry!" Alex said as she playfully went after Carly.

Reese just smiled.

†

They all had a wonderful day. Alex waited downstairs while Reese put Carly to bed. The child had been exhausted and had fallen asleep while watching *The Lion King*. Reese was going to come back down for coffee and dessert after Carly was settled.

Alex had told Reese she could use the bedroom across from hers for Carly. It had been Teddy's room. Reese had not asked but Alex knew that tonight was probably the night for a lot of talking. She heard Reese coming down the stairs and turned to meet those blue eyes. She could tell that Reese was full of questions, but to her credit, she smiled and walked over to her without asking a single one.

Reese." She put her arms protectively around herself as she began to sob again.

This time the sobbing was different, more intense. Alex began to shake and Reese came up from behind and held her.

"I remember thinking how the baby would alter all my plans. I…I actually considered having an abortion…" When she said that her whole body shook with uncontrollable sobbing.

They both slid to the floor, and Reese held on tightly to Alex.

"Oh, God, Reese, that's what kept going through my mind when I saw him, lying on that slab in the hospital. I had wanted to kill my beautiful boy, and I was being punished. My baby was taken away from me…my baby was taken away from me…"

Alex was inconsolable, her sobs filled with more pain than Reese could ever imagine. She knew that nothing she could say at that moment would stop the tears and that Alex needed to shed those tears.

Reese cried with her. She felt the pain that Alex had been holding inside her all these years. She held Alex close and cried with her, sharing her pain.

During the night, they moved to the sofa and Alex fell asleep partially on Reese. Reese was incredulous of how any human being could have held so much pain inside.

Alex clung to Reese even in her sleep. Reese looked down on the dark-haired woman whose face was on her breast and she caressed her hair. Reese cried again with tears of sadness for the woman she loved. Alex carried so much hurt and guilt inside her that it was no wonder she had separated herself from the whole world. She was afraid of the pain. She was so afraid of the pain that loving brought with it. Reese kissed the top of Alex's head and her arms protectively held her a little tighter.

Alex reflexively tightened her hold as well.

Reese wondered how it would have been to know the old Alex. She recalled a conversation with Kate in which Kate had said that Alex had once been joyful and full of life. The Alex in her arms only gave so much, only showed so much, and only felt so much. This Alex was filled with uncertainties and vulnerabilities. She had not realized just how fragile Alex was until tonight. And at that moment, Reese loved her ever so much more.

Reese was filled with a need to protect her, love her, and be there for her. She would always be there to hold Alex. However, this also showed her that Alex might never love her back. She might never want to take the risk. And Reese cried because in finding Alex she now knew she might never truly be hers.

†

It was almost dawn when Alex's eyes opened slowly. She woke feeling a sense of safety and love. She raised her head a little and saw Reese, who held her during the night as she shed all the tears she had been holding in for so long. She looked at the woman's face before her and was filled with a sense of awe.

Reese was a true enigma to Alex. All she had ever asked of Alex was friendship. How could Alex have ever thought that she could just walk out of her life? Alex accepted the fact that her life would not be the same without her in it. Somehow, Reese had brought some peace back into her life. And Alex needed peace. Peace was something she had lost so many, many years ago.

Reese gave her a sense of balance and security. Her friends, her family, her colleagues all thought that she was so in control, when really she was always filled with fear. They all thought she was so strong when she always felt vulnerable and weak. They did not see her, but Reese had. Alex knew that was the thing that frightened her the most. Reese saw her. Reese saw it all, and she knew enough not to force her or push her.

*How had this happened? Somehow this woman holding me, comforting me, loving me...*and at that thought, she stopped.

Reese loved her. Alex was filled with this knowledge, and looked at Reese's face differently. Suddenly, she was filled with both fear and curiosity. Alex studied the face in front of her and noticed every small detail. She remembered the day she had first seen Reese and thinking that she had been beautiful. But looking at her now, Alex realized she had not really seen just how beautiful she was.

This woman holding her filled her with fear but at the same time gave her a sense of being whole; Alex had gotten used to walking around with this empty hole inside her, but Reese somehow made her feel complete. Yes, that is what Reese made her feel. And for the first time since she could remember, Alex didn't think. She allowed herself, at least for that moment in her life, to do what she felt instinctively she needed to do—she reached a hand up to Reese's face and caressed it.

Reese's eyes opened slowly and she leaned into Alex's touch. Blue and green eyes met and no words were needed. Alex's face came closer and her lips went to meet the lips that opened slightly waiting for hers. All she allowed herself to do was feel.

Reese woke up to love touching her, love looking into her eyes, and love's lips kissing her.

Both women slowly gave themselves to the sensuality of the kiss. Both were filled with a sudden hunger as a flame of desire was born. Reese's arms tightened, pulling Alex closer to her.

Alex moved so that she was lying completely on top of Reese. She was filled with a need to possess…she wanted and that was all that her brain registered. She wanted to touch, to feel, to kiss, and to caress. She wanted to make love to Reese. And as the thought registered, her head went up. Whereas a moment before she was filled with need, now she was filled with fear and it showed in her eyes.

Reese saw it. She did not completely release Alex but did loosen her hold on her. She chose to neither acknowledge nor deny that perhaps this moment might bring them closer rather than separating them. She used all the strength in her to allow the woman she loved the time she needed.

Reese smiled. "Good morning," she said simply. "Feeling a little better?" Her voice was gentle as she lovingly put a strand of Alex's hair behind her ear.

"Yes, thank you," answered Alex, her eyes filled with fear and uncertainty. She looked down trying to hide it.

"How about I make us some breakfast in that beautiful unused kitchen of yours?"

Alex looked up and was met with playful, smiling eyes, and she smiled back. "I am starving."

"Good, let's get up and I will make you my famous eggs," Reese said as they both got up from the sofa. "If you have anything in that refrigerator of yours, that is."

"Hey, I have food in there!" Alex walked behind Reese into the kitchen.

"Yeah, sure, you have food in there because we bought it yesterday. I swear I don't know how you don't starve!"

"That's because I eat at your house," Alex answered playfully.

"Oh, so that's why you come over, huh? Because I feed you?" she said, pretending to be mad.

"You found out my secret."

"Yeah, yeah, yeah," said Reese.

Reese started going through the cupboards, and then went to look inside the refrigerator. "God, Alex, you really don't have any food here!" She turned to look at her friend.

"I haven't really lived here for a long time." Alex had a look of sadness again. Reese walked over to her and was unable to stop herself. She kissed Alex lightly on the lips and surrounded her with her embrace.

"You don't have to be afraid, Alex. You are not alone anymore." As she said this, her embrace tightened. And to her surprise, Alex's arms went around her.

"Mommy?"

Both women turned and saw Carly rubbing her eyes. Reese let go of Alex and walked over to her little girl, and Carly's arms went up to her. Reese picked her up and held her tightly to her.

"Good morning, my sweet girl," she said, giving the little girl a squeeze.

Alex smiled at the vision in front of her.

"Good morning, Mommy," replied a sleepy Carly.

"You hungry?"

"Uh-hum." Carly looked toward Alex. "Hi, Alex," she said and held her hand out. Alex walked over and was surprised as Carly put her hands out to her and went into her arms. The little girl buried her face in Alex's neck and her arms went around her shoulders.

Alex felt the same sense of rightness as she had with Reese only minutes before. She looked up and Reese was smiling back at her.

"I'll make us some coffee, okay," she said to Alex with an understanding smile.

"She fell asleep again," said Alex, looking down at Carly and then back at Reese.

"She loves you, Alex. She feels safe with you."

Alex opened her mouth to say something and closed it again. She looked down at the sleeping child in her arms and held her tighter as she kissed her golden head. "I love her too, Reese, I love her too." Alex held Carly lovingly and she began to rock her slowly sideways.

Reese just smiled and went to make the coffee.

Chapter 5

Elliot walked into Alex's office and found her staring out the window, completely unaware that he was even in the room.

"What are you daydreaming about, Counselor?" he said half-jokingly.

Alex turned. Her face looked quite serious and far away before the usual smile was put in place. Elliot knew that smile immediately. It had developed slowly. It was the smile that made people think all was fine when it really wasn't.

"Hello, Elliot," she replied, while going to sit in her chair behind her desk. "You in here to drive me crazy as usual?"

"No, actually, yes. I have the file on that contamination case, and I want your opinion on it. We go to trial in three weeks."

"I will have that for you by Wednesday, all right?" she answered, jotting down a note on her calendar.

"Wednesday?" Elliot grimaced in disbelief that Alex would need that much time. "I don't think it will take you that long. I planned on having your notes by Monday morning."

"I have plans for the weekend. I won't be coming in," she answered, not looking up at Elliot.

"Okay, you have finally said it. Now will you fill me in and tell me what has been changing you. Not that I don't like it," he said before she could protest. Continuing, he said, "Alex, you have looked more alive these last couple of months than I have seen you in the past few years. To what do we owe this change? Who are you seeing? Do I know him?"

"Elliot! Stop! I am not seeing anyone. I am spending time with a friend and her daughter."

Elliot sat down in the chair in front of her desk, looking puzzled. "Oh? I thought...well...never mind. Who is this friend of yours?"

"You met her, she came in here a few months ago," Alex answered, avoiding looking at Elliot.

"I did? Which one?"

"Reese Owens, the blonde woman that came to my office…" she trailed off while she tried going through some papers in front of her.

"The blonde…yes, I remember her. Beautiful woman. She has a daughter, huh?"

"Yes, her daughter's name is Carly. Sweet little thing." Alex still could not look Elliot in the eye. He had known her for too long and Alex did not want to answer questions, nor did she wish to even think about them.

"So, what will you be doing?" he asked innocently enough.

"What is this, the inquisition?" asked an annoyed Alex as she faced a totally confused Elliot.

"What is bothering you? I simply asked a very innocuous question. Jesus, Alex! It's not like you are dating her or anything!" he said mockingly.

Standing up, Alex just stared at him.

Elliot stared back and suddenly sat back down slowly, not losing eye contact with Alex. "Alex, are you seeing her?" he asked softly.

Alex wanted to deny the implication but at that moment, she asked herself the same question. *Am I?* She wasn't sure of her actions or her feelings where

Reese was concerned. She didn't want to see what was happening. Now Elliot had asked and she didn't know quite how to answer.

"Alex?"

She looked away.

"Elliot, I like spending time with her. She makes me feel lighthearted. I don't have to think when I am with Reese. She's fun and active; she and Carly have somehow just filled some of the empty spaces, that's all," she answered. "I enjoy their company."

"All right, Alex. I didn't mean to imply anything." He seemed embarrassed by his assumption.

"Would it have mattered to you if it had been more than friendship, Elliot?" She knew she should just have left it alone and yet she had to know the answer to her question.

"What? If you were dating a woman? I guess it would for a while. I mean, it would certainly be a surprise, but I would still be your friend, Alex."

"Thank you, Elliot," she said with a smile.

"Hey, I almost forgot. I need a date for the Carlton Awards Dinner. So how about it? Are you going with someone?"

"No, I don't have anyone. Sure, we can go to-gether," she replied, eyeing the papers on her desk again.

"Great, it's a date. Shall I pick you up?"

"Sure, sounds fine."

"Well, I'll let you get back to your files." With that, he left her office.

As soon as the door closed, Alex rolled her eyes up to the ceiling. What had she gotten herself into? She had accepted a date with Elliot. Her fingers went through her hair. He had asked her every year to go with him to that stupid awards dinner and she had always said no. And now she had accepted because…why? *Why did I say yes?*

†

After the third ring, Reese picked up the phone. She had run into the house with her briefcase to catch it.

"Hello?" she said, a little out of breath.

"Hey, are you okay, kiddo?"

"Hi, Kate. Just came in through the door."

"Sorry."

"It's okay, Kate. What's up?"

"I thought you guys would like to come over this Saturday for a barbecue and a jump in the pool. Rob is making his famous sautéed chicken. Don't worry, we all usually survive Rob's grilling," she finished saying with a laugh.

Reese laughed in return. "Count us in. Carly loves to play with Kevin."

"Tell my sister that we can make a whole day of it and then we, the adults, can maybe go out to see a movie later on. I have a sitter for the night."

"Sounds great. Hey, why don't you ask her yourself?"

"Reese, she practically lives at your house. I wish she would just move in and get all this over and done with."

Reese was silent. She had not realized how observant Kate was. She thought she was so controlled about her feelings and yet here was Kate commenting on their relationship. She had to admit she was glad that Alex's sister approved.

"Reese? Are you there?" asked Kate. "Look, Reese, I'm not blind, my sister may be but not me."

"Kate…"

"You're good for her. She doesn't know how much yet but she will," Kate said to a very misty-eyed Reese.

"Does it show that much?"

"Honey, you could see it for miles. I knew the minute I saw you two covered in mud," she answered, laughing.

"And you are okay with this, Kate? With me?"

"You are a great person, Reese. Alex is very lucky to have had love find her at last."

"Kate, we are not together in any way…honestly. I wish we were, but we aren't."

"No way! But I thought…the way she looks at you I thought…" Kate said in an incredulous voice.

"No."

"Listen, Reese, Alex has been through hell but she is not blind. She will see it. Don't give up on her. I know she has feelings for you. I can see it every time she looks at you," Kate said, trying to reassure Reese.

"I hope you're right, Kate. I love her more than I can bear sometimes," she answered in a sad voice.

"She will; give her time, Reese. My sister may be

slow, but she is not stupid." She laughed again. "So you will talk to her about Saturday?"

"Yes, I will. And, Kate?"

"Yes?"

"Thank you."

†

After she had finished at the office, Alex was driving as usual toward Reese's house. She pulled up in front of the house and just sat in her car. She asked herself so many questions. Mostly, how had she gotten here and what was she doing coming here every day? It had been a week since she and Reese had last kissed. And she had to admit, she had thought about it a lot. When Elliot asked if she was she seeing her, she had quickly answered no. Is that why she had accepted Elliot's invitation to that awards dinner on Saturday? She was so confused she didn't know what to do or think.

To think of it, she wasn't dating Reese. They were just friends. And friends kissed, didn't they? They had no commitment and for God's sake, Reese was a woman. These questions were ridiculous. Weren't they? And yet, every time she remembered waking up to those blue eyes, she remembered Reese's mouth.

She had never thought of women this way. She had never really thought much about sex, if the truth be told. She just figured that what she had read and heard about the allure of sex was a lot of exaggeration. She couldn't possibly be attracted to Reese.

I'm just not attracted to women period. And on that note, she got out of her car and walked to Reese's house.

†

"Hi there," said Alex as she walked into the kitchen.

"Hi," said Reese with the most beautiful smile Alex had ever seen.

Yes, I have to admit, Reese is beautiful, but I can admire that without... She then looked around, avoiding Reese's eyes.

"Where's Carly?"

"She has Girl Scouts. They started today, re-member?" Reese opened the refrigerator door. "Want a Coke?"

"Yes, thanks," said Alex as she sat down on the stool next to the island in the kitchen.

Reese got out a Coke and put it in front of Alex. "Kate wants to know if we want to go over there on Saturday. Apparently Rob is basting." She laughed. "Oh, and we adults can go to the movies in the evening, Kate has arranged for a sitter." When there was no answer, Reese who was taking some-thing out of the cupboard, turned and looked at the woman. "Alex?"

"Sounds great. You and Carly should go. I have a dinner to go to on Saturday," she answered. Alex kept looking at her soda and not at Reese.

"Oh…I didn't know you had plans…" Reese trailed off.

"Yes, Elliot asked me to go to the Carlton Awards Dinner with him and I accepted. It's this Saturday." Alex still did not look up at Reese.

Reese felt like someone had hit her hard in the chest. She stood rooted to the spot she was standing in. *Alex has a date. Alex is going out with someone else.   Alex   will   be   kissed   goodnight. Alex...Alex...Alex.* She wasn't sure how long she stood in silence in front of Alex.

Alex never looked up.

Finally, Reese spoke. "I see...well, I hope you have a good time, Alex," she said softly and turned around before Alex looked up.

Alex drank her Coke in silence as Reese pretended that she didn't care.

After a few awkward moments, Alex looked up. Something inside her made her want to walk over to Reese and take her in her arms, but instead of doing that, she tried engaging her in conversation. "So, how was school today?"

"The usual. We had teacher in-service today. You know, it's like a workshop for teachers," she answered.

"Sounds interesting. So when will you get your second graders back?"

"Next week. They're thinking of offering Spanish to the teachers as well as adding it to the curriculum."

"You interested in taking a language?"

"Of course I'm interested in learning, Alex. I'm a teacher," she answered louder than she had meant to.

Alex stared at her as they were both facing each other now.

Alex could not avoid noticing the tears welling up in Reese's eyes. She looked down at the Coke can in her hands. "I'm sorry," she said softly.

"Why?"

Alex looked up. "Why what?"

"Why is it so hard for you to love me?" she asked as tears ran down her face. Reese had tried so hard so many times to hide her feelings for Alex, telling herself that she would be satisfied just being Alex's friend. But it wasn't enough anymore. All that filled her mind was so many lonely nights; so many days wanting and not being able to express how much she loved her; so much to say and never able to say a loving word or be able to give a loving touch. It all welled up inside her and she turned her back to Alex, unable to look at her anymore. Reese's hands covered her face as she began to sob. Her body shook with the tears.

Alex sat watching her until she could no longer stand it. She walked over to Reese and tried taking her in her arms.

"Don't!" Reese said, pushing her away.

"Let me hold you!" She had not expected this reaction.

"No! Go away, Alex. Please go away…it hurts to love you." She broke down into tears again.

"Reese…" Alex said softly.

"I thought I could do it, Alex, but I can't. I hoped that you would someday… Please go, Alex." She stood with her back to Alex, leaning on the counter in front of her.

"Reese, I don't want to go," Alex said softly.

"But, do you want to stay, Alex?" Reese asked as she turned around.

Alex gave no answer.

"There is the difference between us. I am not running like you!" she yelled.

"I am not running. I just can't give you what you want!" Alex yelled back.

"And what do I want, Alex? What do you think I want?"

Both women stood looking at one another.

Alex broke eye contact first. "I don't know what you want," she finally said.

"Don't you?" Reese asked softly. "Don't you, Alexandra? I want you. You are what I want."

Alex stared, unable to speak.

Reese moved closer, and when Alex did not move away, her arms went around Alex's neck. She felt Alex's intake of breath as their bodies melded together. Reese's hand went up to Alex's hair and caressed it, finally putting a lock behind her ear.

Alex was spellbound. All she felt was the warmth radiating from Reese's body. All she could hear was a roar in her ears. Her heart pounded in her chest so hard she thought it might burst out of her. *Reese* was all her mind kept saying. All her senses were flooded with her need for Reese. When Reese's mouth came closer, Alex did not wait. Her mouth went out to meet it.

Alex's hands traveled over Reese's body, her mouth wanting more. She could not pull Reese close enough to her. That flame that had once been lit inside her became a raging fire. She was engrossed in her need to touch, to feel, to taste. *Reese.*

Reese only knew her need for Alex. Her hands went through Alex's hair before one traveled down her back. She held her breath as Alex's mouth kissed down her neck toward her breast.

Alex was filled with wanton desire. If she did not touch Reese, she would burn. She wanted Reese's skin. As her mouth traveled down Reese's neck her hands went down her back, over her bottom and she pulled her even closer to her. She could hear Reese's ragged breathing and, as she pulled her to her, she heard the moan that escaped Reese's mouth.

"Oh Alex…"

A persistent ringing finally became audible to both of them.

"What is that?"

"The doorbell…" answered a panting Reese.

"Who...?" Alex asked, trying to catch her breath.

"Oh God, it's Rose…she's dropping Carly off," said Reese as their foreheads touched while they each tried to catch their breath.

The doorbell rang again.

"I better go…" She tried pulling out of Alex's embrace.

Alex pulled her back in her arms again, smiling before lightly kissing her lips and then releasing her.

Reese smiled and blushed. She was straightening her hair and her blouse as she went to answer the door.

Alex lost her smile as Reese walked away.

†

As Reese was talking to her friend Rose, Carly ran into the house.

"Alex!" she screamed, running into Alex's open arms.

Alex scooped up the little girl and twirled her around.

"Hey, small fry. How was Girl Scouts? Did you like it?" she asked as she smiled indulgently at the child in her arms.

"Yep, it was fun. We're going on a camping trip. Want to come, Alex?"

"Wow, a camping trip, huh."

"Yep, with bears and all that stuff," the little girl said seriously, nodding her head.

"Wow, real bears?"

"Yes, that is why we have to practice all these safety things and stuff," she explained.

"What is this I hear about a camping trip?" asked a laughing Reese.

"Alex, is going to come," Carly told her.

"Hey, now wait a minute, small fry. I never said…" Alex stopped as soon as she saw the dejected look on Carly's face.

"Honey, Alex may not like camping," Reese said, trying to reason with the forlorn-looking child.

Carly remained silent, looking down on the floor.

Alex kept looking from Carly to Reese.

"Carly, honey, Alex has to work," Reese said gently as she took Carly from Alex's arms.

Alex felt quite empty all of a sudden. "Hey, wait a minute, small fry, I didn't exactly say *no*," she stuttered.

Carly's head shot up with a hopeful smile.

Reese was looking at her as well.

"Does that mean you will come too?" she asked excitedly.

"That means I will try. If your mom doesn't mind…" Alex trailed off looking at Reese, who smiled at her.

"I would like it too, Alex," said Reese.

Alex smiled in return.

"Hooray we're all going camping!" exclaimed a happy Carly.

"Does this mean I have to sleep in a tent...outdoors…in the woods?" Alex began to look worried. Reese shook her head and started laughing after seeing Alex's concerned expression.

†

For the next few days, they simply fell back to the old routine. It was as if both of them were afraid of scaring the other away. Alex would come over every night, and all three of them would have dinner, watch some television or play board games. Alex would then say goodnight kiss and hug Carly, then kiss Reese goodbye on the cheek.

By Thursday, Alex had not yet broken her date with Elliot. *What am I waiting for?* she asked herself. Her thoughts were interrupted by Carol's voice on the intercom. "Ms. Masters, it's your sister on two."

"Thank you, Carol," said Alex as she picked up the receiver.

"Yes, Katherine?"

"Why so formal?" asked Kate playfully.

"Not formal…what do you want, Kate?" Alex asked in more relaxed tone.

"Just checking on Saturday. I spoke with Reese and she wasn't sure about it. Alex, she sounded a little funny when I asked. Did anything happen?" Kate asked.

"I have a date with Elliot," she simply said.

"You what?"

"I have accepted Elliot's invitation to an awards dinner on Saturday."

There was no answer from Kate.

"Hey! You still there?" Alex asked.

"Alex…I don't know quite what to say," Kate said, sounding miffed.

"There is nothing to say."

"Alex, are you sure you want to do this?" asked Kate carefully.

"What do you mean?"

"Oh, Alex, cut the shit okay? I have eyes, and I see how you look at Reese," Kate finally said.

"I…"

"Alex, be careful you don't lose what you have been given. Love is a gift, Alex."

This time it was Alex who did not answer.

"Goodbye, Alexandra. Be happy with your conventions and your appearances," Kate said sarcastically.

"That is not fair, Kate!" Alex exclaimed.

"No, it's not. Sometimes we have love for only a little while. Don't waste it, Alex. I guess…I just don't want you to let it pass you by," said Kate in a sad-sounding voice. "Think about that, Alex," she said before hanging up.

As Alex hung up, she was enveloped by her thoughts. Reese had not asked about Saturday again after their…their conversation in the kitchen that night. How would Reese react if Alex were to go out with Elliot on Saturday? Why was she going with Elliot on Saturday was the real question.

†

On Friday night, they acted as if it were any other night. Alex kissed Carly and hugged her good night. Reese walked her to the door as usual. Alex turned to kiss her goodbye but was stopped by the look in Reese's eyes.

Both women stood for a moment just looking at each other, before Alex broke eye contact first. Reese took a step forward and kissed Alex lightly on the lips and then pulled away.

"Good night, Alex," she said softly.

Alex looked up and was once again mesmerized with those beautiful blue eyes. She took a step forward and then just as quickly pulled back. "Goodnight, Reese," Alex said softly as she turned and walked away.

Chapter 6

"Hi, Reese, come on in," said Kate with a smile. "Carly, sweetheart, I love that pink outfit!"

"Thank you, Mrs. Stenbeck," said Carly politely.

"I brought a chocolate mousse cake for dessert," Reese told Kate as she and Carly walked into the house.

"God, I love you!" Kate exclaimed.

"What is it with your family and this chocolate fetish?" Reese asked, laughing. "I swear Alex pants for chocolate."

"You should know," Kate said laughingly at Reese.

"I wish," answered Reese dejectedly.

Kate looked back at her in dismay. "Carly, honey, Kevin is already in the pool. Why don't you go ahead and jump in? The water is just perfect."

"Mommy, can I?" Carly implored.

"Rob is back there supervising."

"Okay, Carly honey, but listen to Mr. Stenbeck, okay?"

"Okay, Mommy," Carly said as she went running toward the sliding doors that led to the pool.

"Don't run, Carly!"

Carly stopped running and looked back. "Sorry."

Kate looked toward Reese. "Isn't Alex coming?" she asked Reese.

Reese looked forlorn. "I don't know, Kate. Last night we just said good night and that was it. I didn't want to push too hard."

"Oh, Reese, I'm sorry," Kate said, trying to comfort her.

"She never promised me anything, Kate. I have no right to expect anything from her."

"So nothing has happened at all?" Kate asked, hoping that Alex had made some kind of move, but it seemed that her sister was still in the slow lane.

"Well, not exactly nothing…" Reese trailed off.

"What? What?" Kate asked excitedly.

"Well…we had the most passionate kiss I have ever had in my life in the kitchen the other day. If the doorbell hadn't…well, who can say?" Reese's face went from a smile back to a disappointed expression.

"I swear, Alexandra can go from brilliant to downright stupid sometimes," said Kate in exasperation.

"Maybe she just doesn't like me enough like that…"

"Yeah right!" exclaimed a disbelieving Kate.

"I don't know, Kate. Maybe I should just try to put this behind me and allow both Alex and I to move on. It's making me miserable. And Alex…well Alex may just need a friend not a lover."

"I'm sorry, Reese. She is the loser in this," Kate said as they both walked out to the pool.

†

The dinner was noisy. They had finished with the awards and now the music was playing loudly.

"Want to dance, Alex?" asked Elliot.

"Sure, why not," said Alex, getting up.

They walked to the dance floor and Alex moved into Elliot's arms. *He is a good dancer*, she thought as she started swaying to the music. As her body started to relax, thoughts of Reese gradually started encompassing her mind.

She remembered clearly how it had felt holding Reese in her arms. Kissing Reese, smelling her, how her mouth and her embrace felt... She realized Elliot had been talking to her and she shook her head trying to clear it.

Confused, he said to her, "What? I thought you liked the ocean?"

"Oh...I'm sorry, Elliot. I wasn't listening. What did you say again?"

That set the trend for the rest of the night. She would drift off and Reese would fill her thoughts. When Elliot suggested they leave, she jumped at it. Finally, the night was over and Alex found herself thinking that tomorrow was Sunday and she would see Reese.

Elliot drove her home and walked her to the door.

"Thank you, Elliot. I had a nice time," she said. As she was pulling her hand away, he took her in his arms and kissed her. Alex, caught by surprise, froze on the spot. When she was about to pull away he released her and smiled. Alex just stared at him.

"Goodnight, Alex. Thank you. I had a wonderful time too," he said with a huge smile on his face. He then turned around and walked away. Elliot got into his car, waved, and drove away while Alex still stood in the same spot staring after him.

She finally turned around and went inside.

✝

Alex tossed and turned all night. She finally just got up and went down to the kitchen for a glass of milk. Getting a glass out of the cupboard she poured herself a glass of chocolate milk then walked over to the table and sat down. The milk made her feel better and, as she was about to finish, she got up and walked over to her study to check her answering machine. Maybe Reese had left a message.

She touched the button that was blinking. There was one message left from Kate at ten that night.

God, Alex, I hope you know what you are do-ing! We all had a nice time here. The kids had a ball in the pool and then we all went to the movies. Reese is a great person, and you, my dear sister, are an idiot. I think you went a little too far today. I hope it didn't cost you your happiness. Sometimes, Alex...well, call me tomorrow. Bye, Alex.

The machine beeped twice and that was the message.

What did Kate mean? She knew exactly what Kate meant. She wished that Kate would just stay out of this. She and Reese were just friends. Well, maybe a little more than friends since they had kissed…the enormity of the emotion that one kiss had produced was still very much on her mind.

Alex went back up to bed and spent the rest of the night tormented by Kate's message and visions of Reese.

When she finally woke later Sunday morning, she felt tired and her head felt groggy. After taking a shower and making some coffee, she took her cup into the study and tried to call Reese. After the fifth ring, Alex stared at the handset as if it were an alien object. She looked over at the clock on her desk. It said ten o'clock. *Where is Reese?* She dialed again, thinking maybe she had dialed the number incorrectly. Again no answer.

Alex started pacing. Where was Reese? Why hadn't she told her she was going out today? *Why should she have to tell me?* the little voice in her head said. Alex kept calling every hour until the early part of the evening. She had not eaten or done anything but sit in the chair behind her desk in the study. Her only motion was picking up the phone every hour, on the hour, and dialing Reese's number.

When seven o'clock came around, she got up, grabbed her car keys, got in her car and headed toward Reese's house.

Suppose something has happened to her? That had to be the reason she was not at home. *No, why would something have happened?* When she pulled into Reese's driveway a car almost immediately pulled in behind her. She got out and waited next to her car.

Reese got out of the passenger's side and smiled at her. Alex looked over at the driver of the car. When the driver's door opened a young woman with luscious auburn hair got out, she glanced at Reese then turned around to help Carly out of the backseat.

"Hi, Alex," Reese said.

Alex kept looking at the dark-haired woman as she went to get some bags out of the trunk of the car. Alex then looked to where Reese was standing.

"Hi," she said crisply.

"I wasn't expecting you. This is Gail. We are going to make some quesadillas. Would you like to stay for dinner?" Reese asked.

Alex was silent. Reese looked over to Gail whose arms were filled with grocery bags.

"Alex!" exclaimed Carly as she ran into Alex's arms.

"Hi, small fry," Alex said, smiling at the child.

"Gail is making some quesadillas. Do you like them?" the small child asked.

"Sure," answered Alex, looking over to Reese and Gail.

As they all headed inside the house Alex noticed the way Gail was looking at Reese. She decided right there and then that she didn't like her. She didn't like Gail one bit.

†

It had been two weeks since Gail had come into Alex's picture-perfect world. It started gradually. First, she noticed the usual phone calls to her office from Reese begin to lessen. Then a week after this change Reese called to tell her that she would be busy one, then two nights. Slowly it was changing and Alex started to panic.

She felt odd, somehow, walking into Reese's house where before she had just come in. Reese had given her a key and asked her to just use it and let herself in when she had started coming by every day after she finished at the office. Now, it felt strange and she was beginning to feel like a visitor. Something had changed after that weekend when she went out with Elliot and Reese went out with Gail. Every day she felt Reese pulling away a little more. And Alex felt the absence of her more and more every day.

She missed the intimacy and the feeling of belonging. They didn't even kiss goodnight anymore. Reese was pushing her away. *Why should this bother me?* They were still friends…not like before, but still friends. If she didn't want a more physical relationship with Reese, then she should be happy. But, Alex realized, she wasn't…she wasn't happy at all.

†

A week later, it all came apart. When Reese called her to break the plans they had made for the weekend, Alex realized she had lost something very precious. She had lost the joy she had found in Reese and Carly and this terrified her. Hanging up the phone after talking to Reese, she stood, her back against the wall and slid to the floor, covering her mouth as a sob escaped. The darkness began to close her in as Alex cried into the night.

†

112

It had been four days since she had last spoken to Reese. Alex was sullen and the hardness that had started to leave her features had begun to reappear again.

"Ms. Masters, Reese Owens on line four," Carol's voice came over the intercom. Alex leaned back on her chair and remained silent. "Ms. Masters?"

"Tell her…I am not available, Carol," she said into the intercom and went back to her paperwork.

†

Reese called every day for the remainder of the week, and Alex was always unavailable. Alex had begun to feel the cold slide itself back into her life. Her days were filled with work and more work.

Elliot had been dispatched out of her office after she had picked a fight over something totally banal. Alex had told him off in no uncertain terms. Slowly she was going back to the life she had thought she had left behind.

After two weeks, Reese stopped calling.

One night, Alex pulled into her driveway, went into an empty house and closed the door.

Quite suddenly, she started to shake.

What has happened? she asked, looking around her house. All she could see was the emptiness; all she could hear was the silence. She braced herself and went into the living room. She opened the decanter filled with thirty-year-old scotch, poured herself a glass and gulped it down. She then proceeded to refill it then walked over to the sofa and sat down while she drank the contents of the second glass.

She wasn't sure how long she had been sitting in the dark when the doorbell rang. The incessant buzzing made her get up, walk over to the front door, and pull it open.

"What!" she yelled as she swung the door open. Her expression changed completely when she saw Reese standing in front of her.

Alex stood in stunned silence. *Reese!* her mind whispered tentatively. Reese stood in front of her. All she had to do was reach out and she could touch her, hold her, kiss her...

"Are you going to let me in or do you hate me that much?" Reese asked angrily.

"Come in," Alex answered just as sarcastically.

Reese walked in past her. "Well, can we turn on the lights or are you living literally in the dark too?" Reese snapped as she turned around to face Alex. Alex slammed the door shut.

They both stood in the dark, illuminated by the diffused lighting coming through the glass panels on the sides of the door, creating a soft glow around them. The air was so charged that it kept them physically apart.

Alex relented, and reached out to flick the light switch up. She walked back into the living room followed by Reese. She went directly to the scotch decanter and poured herself another drink. She swallowed it, took a deep breath, and turned to face Reese. "Want some?" Alex asked, showing her the empty glass.

"Drinking won't make it go away," Reese said softly.

Alex shook her head and looked down at the glass in her hand. "It dulls what ails you," she answered as if talking to herself.

Reese was not about to let her wallow in self-pity. "Why have you been avoiding me? You haven't taken my phone calls. You haven't come around the house. You have simply just cut me out of your life and thrown me out with the trash," Reese accused her angrily.

Alex's head snapped up as she turned back and started filling her glass again.

Reese was suddenly next to her and snatched the glass out of Alex's hand, spilling the gold liquid all over.

"What are you doing?" Alex demanded irritably, taking the glass back.

"I am…I am here, Alex." Reese suddenly sounded tired. "I am here, loving you." Reese's eyes met Alex's wounded ones.

Alex walked away from her and the silence stood between them. "Where's Gail?" Alex demanded without turning to look at Reese.

"Probably where I left her, in bed!"

Alex turned to face Reese with a scowl on her face. Suddenly, Alex closed the distance between them and grabbed Reese by both arms and shook her. "Why are you here? Are you trying to drive me crazy?" she growled, looking into Reese's eyes accusingly.

"Why should it matter to you who I sleep with as long as it isn't you?" Reese yelled back.

"How could you let her touch you? How could you let her kiss you after me?" she demanded angrily.

"After you!" exclaimed Reese as she pulled herself out of Alex's grip. "After you? I don't belong to you. You don't want me, remember?" Reese's eyes filled with tears and the pain inside her was visible.

"Get out! Get out!" Alex yelled.

Alex just stared at Reese when she didn't move.

The tears started rolling down Reese's face and she started to speak softly. "You don't want me, Alex. She does. She looks at me the way I wish you would. She wants all that you don't. And I…I sent her away because all I want is you." Reese took in a deep breath before she continued. Alex just stood and stared. "I never slept with her, Alex. I am in love with you." Reese's voice shook with crying. "Why are you fighting me so hard? Is it so terrible to love me?"

Alex did not answer and the silence grew between them.

Finally, Reese spoke. "I am cursed with loving you, wanting you, dreaming of you, crying for you. Do you know that, Alex? I have been reduced to crying for you. I'm not ashamed to tell you because loving someone is beautiful. I don't care what the world thinks. All I know is that I love you. I have to put some distance between us because loving you is going to kill me, Alex. I can't live like this. I can't. I won't bother you anymore," Reese finished speaking softly and walked toward the door.

The sound of glass breaking filled the silence. Reese looked back and found Alex still standing in the same place staring at her, the floor beneath her covered by broken glass. "You're running away?" asked an angry Alex.

Reese just stared back. Instead of answering, she just seemed to look sadder.

"You are! You're running away!" exclaimed Alex even louder in disbelief.

Alex quickly closed the distance between them to stand in front of Reese. She was close enough to feel her breathing but did not touch her.

A sob escaped Reese as her head bent down. She swayed into Alex's arms and held her as her crying became audible and her body shook. Suddenly, Alex's arms went around her and pulled her closer.

Alex's embrace quickly got tighter and Reese buried her face in Alex's neck. "Alex," she cried, breathing her in. Reese said her name with a mixture of pain and pleasure. As she was about to pull away, Alex pulled her back into her embrace and her mouth covered Reese's with a need that took her by surprise.

Alex's lips were warm and enticing and Reese gave herself over to the sensations. Alex's lips brushed hers lightly now. "No…don't go…" said Alex before she again covered Reese's mouth with her own.

Alex's kisses demanded with a hunger that caught Reese off guard. She pulled away, trying to catch her breath and stared at Alex in a mixture of surprise and incredulity.

Alex spoke first. "I don't want you to go," she said softly. "I don't want you to go," she repeated. "I need you."

Reese stared in confusion.

"I need you," she said again as she pulled Reese back into her embrace

"Alex," Reese said softly as she tried pulling away from the embrace that held her.

"I'm afraid, Reese," Alex said softly into Reese's hair.

Reese stood still, listening.

Alex continued, "I'm afraid to love you. But, I'm more afraid to lose you..." she trailed off.

Reese kissed Alex's neck tenderly. "I'm here, Alex. I'm here and I want to love you. Let me love you, Alex."

Alex was the one to pull away this time, turning away from Reese.

Reese stopped Alex in her place and looked into such vulnerable eyes. She saw so much raw hurt. She lifted her hand to caress Alex's face. "I won't hurt you, sweetheart," she said softly.

Alex pulled away. "What if I lose you?" She stood with her back to Reese.

Reese came up behind her and turned her around. "I can't promise that I won't die, Alex. I wish I could. But I can't. I do promise to love you till my dying day," she said with all the love possible visible in her eyes. Her hand reached out and caressed Alex's face tenderly. Alex leaned into the caress and her eyes closed as she surrendered to the warmth that seemed to be infiltrating her body. She was tired of fighting Reese, tired of needing the woman, tired of the loneliness and of the time she spent missing Reese, wanting Reese…loving her.

Reese's body was welcoming, and as Alex gave in completely to the embrace she experienced the warmth of surrender. Reese held her close and her body responded, swaying toward the object of its need. "Reese, Reese, I've missed you," she whispered into Reese's ear as one hand went into her hair and the other pulled her even closer. Alex wanted to melt into the woman in her arms.

"Alex, oh Alex," Reese said before her mouth was claimed once more.

Alex pulled away, took her by the hand, and led the way up the stairs.

Reese was filled with both excitement and anticipation. Her breathing became heavy. And she stopped halfway up the stairs, not believing what was happening. She looked toward Alex and was rewarded with the brightest of smiles. Alex stood next to her in the middle of the staircase holding nothing back. Her eyes were completely open and all that Reese could see in them was love mirrored back at her.

Alex kissed her gently at first. And as Reese's mouth responded, the need between the two women intensified.

Reese was now leaning against the wall as Alex's mouth traveled down her neck, and her hands pulled Reese's hips against her.

"Reese, I want to see you," said Alex with a breathless voice so filled with passion that she hardly recognized it as her own.

"Yes, make love to me, Alex," Reese said as she leaned her head back even further.

"Come…" Alex took Reese by the hand again and climbed the remaining steps even faster, leading her into her bedroom. Alex leaned toward the bedside lamp and looked at Reese asking a silent question. When Reese nodded the room filled with soft lighting that glowed with a dream-like haze. Alex walked up to Reese again and their eyes met expressing so much more than words ever could.

Alex pulled Reese to her for a kiss while her hands started pulling Reese's blouse out of her slacks. Breaking the kiss Reese raised her hands and Alex removed the blouse over her head.

Alex never took her eyes away from Reese's. Once Reese unhooked her bra and it fell to the floor, Alex's eyes focused on Reese's breasts. *Oh god, Reese's breasts are perfect,* she thought; they fit so perfectly in her hands and their allure was her undoing. Her mouth opened slightly as her hands caressed them. Alex looked up and saw Reese's eyes closed and her head bent slightly back. Her hands then started caressing lower over Reese's abdomen and then started unbuttoning the slacks.

"Alex…." moaned Reese.

Alex pulled back and Reese's eyes opened. She searched Alex's face, questioning. The awe and admiration visible in Alex's features and then blue eyes met green. For a moment, she saw such vulnerability in those green eyes. Reese, filled with so much tenderness, she quickly filled the space between them and kissed Alex lightly.

"We don't have to do this if you are not ready, we have all the time in the world," she said lovingly to Alex.

Alex's eyes softened. "I am not afraid. I am taking in the moment. I want to remember it forever. You are so beautiful, oh God, you are so beautiful," said Alex without releasing Reese's eyes for one moment.

Reese started to slowly remove Alex's clothing. When she was done, she saw so much love in Alex's eyes that Reese then allowed herself to look down at the body of the woman who had taken over her thoughts and held her heart. Reese stared at Alex's full breasts and her eyes traveled down to perfect hips. She could feel her body reacting to her need to possess Alex. Reese was filled with a desire to tease those breasts and to touch and caress the body of the woman before her.

Neither woman spoke. They instinctively went into each other's arms. Hands caressed and mouths explored as both women fell onto the bed with sweet abandonment.

Alex was on top one minute, then Reese. They could not seem to get close enough.

Alex was above Reese, lifting herself to catch her breath. She stopped and stared at the beautiful woman beneath her and her mouth came down slowly to find the lips she had wanted to kiss from the very first day she had seen her. Slowly, she began to move against the body beneath her, grinding with such pleasure that her moans ascended and grew louder as the emotions inside her built beyond the realm or reason, she reacted only to the need that filled her. All she knew was Reese's skin, the scent of her body that grew to meet and entice all of her senses with a desire that became lost to all reason. All she felt was hunger; a hunger that had been hidden inside her and now would not be denied. Suddenly the flood of emotions filled her body with such power that the release of pleasure was beyond anything she had ever experienced before. There was no control and, for the first time in Alex's life, she allowed herself to just feel and not think.

Reese's release came as well and both women held onto one another in its aftermath.

The air filled with intake of breaths and delicious moans of release and satisfaction. And as the night progressed, bodies moved, lips were kissed and hearts were given and taken.

Chapter 7

The ringing of the telephone next to Alex's bed woke them. Alex's eyes opened in annoyance but her features quickly turned into a smile that reached her eyes as she saw the woman sprawled on top of her. She reached for the handset.

"Hello? This better be good," she said in irritation.

"Alexandra, I want to talk to you!" said a peeved-sounding Kate.

"Not now, Kate."

"Listen, you nitwit! I saw Reese yesterday and that girl deserves better than you," Kate said in indignation.

"I agree with that," said Alex calmly.

"Alex, I mean it. What the hell is wrong with you?"

"Nothing now, sis, nothing at all," she replied with a big smile on her face. She saw a smiling

Reese looking back at her. Alex leaned toward her and kissed her lightly.

"Alex, I'm coming over to knock some sense into you!" exclaimed an irritated Kate.

"Actually, Kate, could we get together tomorrow maybe?" Alex said, trying to hold back her laughter.

"Alex!"

"Hi, Kate," a drowsy Reese said into the receiver after taking it away from Alex.

"Reese?" asked a surprised Kate.

"Yes, it's me, Kate," Reese said with a smile on her face, looking at Alex.

"Okay, we can talk later. Bye."

The air was filled with dial tone.

Reese looked at the telephone in her hand and laughed as she looked at Alex.

"She hung up...I think we scared her," Reese said, smiling at Alex.

Alex reached out and pulled Reese toward her. "Good morning, love," said Alex as she kissed her squarely on the mouth.

"Good morning to you too."

"Breakfast," Alex said as she raised her eyebrows comically, throwing up the sheets and diving underneath.

Reese started to giggle.

†

"How do you like your eggs, Alex? Do you even have any eggs?" Reese asked, leaning into the opened refrigerator. She looked up when she didn't receive an answer. Alex had a funny look on her face.

"What?" asked Reese.

"I love you, you know," answered Alex with a bigger smile.

Reese walked over to her and into her arms. "And no, I don't have any eggs. I don't think I have much of anything in there."

"I'll make us some coffee and then maybe we can have breakfast at my house, after we pick up the small fry from Rose's house, sound good?" Reese suggested.

Alex nodded her head but did not release Reese.

"You planning on hanging on to me?" Reese asked dreamily.

"Forever." Alex's mouth sought out Reese's wonderful, luscious lips and breakfast was forgotten.

✝

"Chicken pox?" Alex exclaimed into the telephone a couple of days later.

"I'm afraid so, honey," was Reese's reply.

"Oh God, no..." said a deflated Alex.

"Have you had them?"

"No," Alex answered.

"Oh no…"

✝

"How long has it been?" Kate asked having stopped at Alex's office after a lunch meeting nearby.

"Seven days, four hours and seventeen minutes," Alex said, looking at her watch.

"Sore subject, huh?" Kate asked with a sorry expression on her face.

"It's a sore subject right now," Alex said, going back to the papers on her desk.

"Are you okay?" Kate was suddenly concerned.

Alexandra looked up and away, looking toward the window. "I...yes, everything is fine." She went back to work on the papers in front of her.

"Alex?"

"Yes, really, all is good. Now let me get back to work. Do you have a life or does it only revolve around mine?" Her tone was joking.

"Alex, you would tell me right?" Kate asked, not allowing Alex to get away with a thing.

Alex got up suddenly and walked toward the window at the corner of her office. She stood in front of it with her back to Kate.

"Everything is supposed to be fine, but it's not Kate."

"What do you mean?"

"You're joking, right?" Alex was facing her now with a surprised look on her face.

"Alexandra, don't do this."

"Don't do what?" Alex threw her hands up in the air.

"You're scared, that's all. It's going to be fine. This separation is unfortunate but, Alex, you love her."

Alex ran her fingers through her hair and suddenly looked tired. She walked over to her desk and sat down in her chair again. "Yes, I'm scared. I'm scared of not being able to handle this. I can just see myself at the partner's dinner saying I'd like to introduce my lover. Yes, she is a woman but don't let that worry you, I'm still the same old Alex. Can you honestly say that it won't matter? Kate…I'm scared. I don't know if I can do this. And I don't know if I can give her up." Alex sounded confused, even to herself.

"Well…I guess the only question is, do you love her?"

Alex looked up and thought for a moment. Suddenly a smile and faraway look filled her face. "Do I love her? Yes, oh yes."

"A step at a time, sis, a step at a time."

†

After Kate had left her office Alex needed the reassurance of Reese's voice so she picked up the telephone and dialed the number that would connect her to what she needed more than breathing at that moment—Reese's voice.

"Hello?"

"Who is this?" Alex asked into the telephone's receiver.

"This is Gail. Who is this?"

"Is Reese there?" Alex asked with suppressed anger.

"Yes, but she's kind of busy right now."

"Will you please get her on the phone?"

"No, I can't, she's in the shower. Alex…right? I'll tell her you called," Gail replied angrily before the line went dead.

Alex slammed the phone down. All that filled her was a sense of betrayal so great that it encompassed all of her. She was filled with a confusion she had never known and the anger building inside her closed her up like a hot iron closed an open wound.

†

The phone had rung several times after she got home, but Alex did not pick up the receiver. She sat in her dark living room with her thirty-year-old scotch. She didn't go in to the office the next day.

†

Two days had passed since Gail answered Reese's phone. It was late afternoon when the door to Alex's office burst open and a very angry blonde marched through, followed shortly by a very upset Carol. "I'm sorry, Ms. Masters…"

"It's okay, Carol, we're old friends," Alex said a smugly. Carol walked out of the office, closing the door behind her.

Reese stood in the same spot, fuming.

"Chicken pox scare over?" Alex asked comically.

"I am not going to play this game with you!" Reese exclaimed with her hands on her hips. She wasn't sure what had happened or why Alex was acting this way but this yes one minute and no the next could not continue.

"I am not playing. It was nice but it's gotten to be a bore." Alex started reading the papers in front of her.

Reese stood there not believing what she had just heard. It felt like someone had hit her and knocked the wind out of her. She stood in shocked silence, unable to speak until Alex looked up at her again.

"I don't believe you," said Reese softly.

"What is there not to believe? We had a good time but it's kind of over, don't you think? You were, shall we say, a great experience." Alex's voice was full of sarcasm.

"Alex, I don't believe you. Why are you doing this?" Reese was shocked.

"Doing what? You wanted me to take you to bed and it was good, I have to give you that." Alex got up, walked over to the front of her desk, and sat on it with her arms crossed in front of her. "You were satisfied too from what I can remember. Yes, I believe you were satisfied quite a few times."

Reese walked up to her and slapped her hard. Alex stood up and grabbed Reese by both arms.

"Don't you ever touch me again," Alex growled between her teeth.

"I hate you!" Reese cried as tears started running down her face.

Alex pulled her closer and kissed her hard on the mouth and just as suddenly released her. "Now, go back to Gail!"

"What are you talking about?" cried a confused Reese.

"I'm really busy, Reese." Alex replied very businesslike.

Reese stood for a moment just staring at the woman she loved. What had happened? This was not her Alex. Had it all truly been a lie? If it was, this was a monster that now stood in front of her.

"I won't ever forgive you, Alex. You used me. I loved you and you used me," said a sobbing Reese accusingly as she ran out of Alex's office.

Alex stood in her empty office for a moment then walked over to the door and closed it. She walked back to her desk, sat down and began to go through her paperwork.

†

Reese could not remember ever hurting so much. How could she have been so wrong? It had all seemed so real. How could she go on without her? She closed her eyes as the tears ran down her cheeks. After a few minutes she started her car and drove home on autopilot.

She pulled into her driveway and went inside the house. She had to get dinner ready. Rose was going to be dropping Carly off after Girl Scouts. It was over. All her plans for a future with Alex were over. She stood in the middle of her kitchen and suddenly collapsed to the floor in tears.

"Oh God, why does it have to hurt so much?" She covered her face and the sobs just came. "Alex…Alex."

†

"Reese, wait up!" Rose yelled.

"Hi, Rose, what's up?" Reese said as Rose came up to her.

"Can you pick up the girls tomorrow? I know it's my turn, but…"

"Sure, not a problem. I'll pick them up and drop off Lindsey at your house."

"Thanks, I'm expecting a delivery tomorrow and you know how they are. They tell you anytime between nine and five. I hate that." They both began walking toward the parking lot. "Hey, you seem kind of preoccupied these days, kiddo."

"Just some things to deal with. But it's okay," Reese said softly.

Rose stopped and Reese looked back at her. "Hey, something is wrong. I didn't want to pry, but are you okay, Reese?"

"I will be, Rose, I will be."

"Mommy!" Carly yelled and Reese opened her arms which were immediately filled with her daughter.

"Hi, small fry." Reese kissed Carly.

"Alex used to call me that," Carly said as Reese gently set her down.

"Well, we better get going." Reese tried to control the tears threatening to spill over. "Bye, Rose, don't worry about tomorrow."

"Okay," Rose replied as she watched Reese and Carly walk away. Rose hadn't known Reese very long but they had grown to be friends quickly. Reese, she thought, was a nice woman trying to raise her daughter on her own like Rose was.

Rose had noticed a change in her friend. Reese was by nature a happy person. For a few months she had really seemed happy and then suddenly, a few months ago, Rose had noticed the difference. Her friend had gotten sad.

Rose knew all about being sad. She remembered how it had been when Paul left. She thought it was going to kill her but it hadn't. Now she saw the same sadness in Reese. She knew people only talked about some things when they were ready and Rose thought Reese was not ready. She wondered, though, if this man called Alex caused Reese's sadness.

She could not remember any Alex that Reese had mentioned, only that girlfriend of hers. She remembered the sadness in Reese's eyes as Carly mentioned Alex. All of a sudden Rose froze. Reese had mentioned her friend before. She remembered the look in Reese's eyes but somehow Rose had not made the connection. Now it all became quite clear.

"Holy shit!"

She shook her head and looked to the parking lot where Reese was putting Carly in the backseat and then getting into her car.

She looks just like anyone one else, Rose thought then quickly chastised herself for the ignorance the thought expressed. *That type of thinking is what she probably has to deal with all the time,* thought Rose, and she felt even sadder for her friend.

Rose gave this new realization a lot of thought and made up her mind to speak to her friend as soon as possible.

†

"Kate, it's September twenty-third today; I don't know what I will be doing for Thanksgiving," Alex said, irritated.

"You know what, Alex? You are getting harder to take on a daily basis. If I didn't love you I would just wash my hands of you," Kate said, sounding just as irritated.

"I'm sorry. I have a lot of paperwork, and I go to trial on a very complex case in a few weeks. I am really swamped, Kate." Alex sounded tired.

"Alex…about Reese…"

"I don't want to discuss Reese, Kate. Don't fight me on this. I will not discuss this with you. Leave it alone, Kate, or I will simply walk out of your life… I didn't mean that, Kate. I just don't want to discuss it, okay?"

"Okay, Alex. You're my sister and I love you. Remember that, okay?" Something awful had happened between Reese and Alex. Neither had wanted to discuss it. And Alex was more withdrawn than ever. But Kate also knew that when Alex got like this there was no talking to her. Something terrible had happened and Alex had just closed all the doors.

"I will try and keep Thanksgiving open okay, Kate? Bye."

"Good, we love you, you know. And we want you there," Kate said softly.

There was silence from the other side of the line and Kate thought she had heard a sob before the line went dead.

What happened? Kate kept asking herself. Alex had come to life for those few months with Reese. She had looked so happy. And for a while she thought Alex and Reese had found something special in each other. Her sister had gotten past all of her doubts with conventions and the what-would-people-say thing. She thought that, finally, Alex would be happy. Then, quite suddenly, it had all gone terribly wrong.

She didn't see Reese much anymore either. She realized Reese had been avoiding her except for the time they met by chance in the supermarket:

"Reese, hi."

"Hello, Kate."

"I have missed you, where have you been keeping yourself?"

"Oh, you know, busy with Carly and everything. How's the family?" Reese seemed to want to change the subject.

"Just fine, starting school. You know how that is."

"Yeah, I do." Reese looked down for a moment. "How is Alex?" she asked softly.

"She's fine. Reese, I really think—"

"No, Kate, but thanks. It was nice seeing you again. Bye."

And Reese walked away looking very sad.

Kate kept asking herself what could have hap-pened. She should just mind her own business, but damn if she would. Alexandra was miserable and so was Reese. Obviously they had not been able to fix it themselves so she would. These two women be-longed together even if she was the only one who thought so for the moment. Kate started working out a plan.

"Yesssss!" yelled an excited Kate.

†

"Thank you so much for picking up the girls from Girls Scouts for me today. Come on in," said Rose.

"Sure, I can stay a minute. The girls are putting their project in the garage." Reese walked into Rose's house.

"Want some coffee?"

"I would love some," answered Reese as they both walked over to the kitchen. "I love what you have done in here, Rose. I like the contrast of the light walls with the cabinets."

"Thanks, I really like the way it came out too. Cream and sugar?"

"Yes, thanks."

Both women sat down at the kitchen table to drink their coffee.

"Reese, there is something I would like to say to you, and I would ask you not to say anything until I say my piece, okay?"

"Okay," Reese answered with a curious expression.

"Reese, I think you are a wonderful teacher." Rose looked at a smiling Reese. "I also think that you are a very nice person. You are also my friend. I want you to know that I will be here for you no matter what, Reese. I think you should tell me about Alex."

Reese's mouth opened and closed. She looked uncomfortable.

"Reese, I know you're gay."

Reese looked up quickly and stared at her friend. What she saw made her eyes fill with tears. "Oh, Rose," she said, putting her hand over her friend's.

"What happened with Alex, Reese?"

Reese hesitated and then looked into the understanding eyes of her friend and started to speak.

Reese cried all the tears she had been holding onto for the past few months. Rose was there and she listened. And Reese realized that in this pain, she had found comfort in Rose's understanding. And for the first time in months, Reese was able to speak of what it had meant to lose her love to another human being. And it felt good to tell it.

†

After having knocked a few times, Elliot poked his head into Alex's office and saw that she was oblivious to all. He walked closer to the desk she was sitting behind and watched as she played with a key in her hand. It occurred to him that he had seen her looking at a key, if not the same one, on more than one occasion and on each of those times, she had been far away as well.

"Key to your heart, Alex?" he asked gently. She looked up noticing him for the first time and then looked down at the key again. Elliot did not expect an answer. She looked at the key a moment longer before putting in back in her drawer and closing it.

"Yes," she replied softly. "The key to my heart." She did not look up.

Elliot found himself without any words. He had known something was wrong. He could no longer understand what was happening with Alex. For a while he thought she might have met someone and then this.

"Alex—" he started to say gently.

"Elliot, as to the fund-raiser on the twelfth, I'll go with you." She sounded more like the Alex he was used to. She looked sure of herself and strong. Had it all been an illusion? What was happening to his friend?

"Okay, great. Will Katherine and Robert be attending as well?" He was all business now.

"They go every year. I don't know who will be at their tables. Rob's company usually buys two to three every year. I'll talk to Kate later today, and then I'll let you know as soon as possible."

"All right, sounds great. I will pass the information on to the Bradleys. This is a great cause.

These funds will keep the children's center open for the next year."

"Yes, it is a wonderful cause. The Bradleys have done wonders for that center. Did you know that they lost their son to leukemia two years ago?"

"No, I didn't know."

"I met him once. He was a very charming little boy. I have become a sponsor this year."

"Alex, that's wonderful!"

She looked up. "Yes, well, I will expect a rather large check from all the partners so pass it along." She gave him a calculating smile.

Elliot shook his head. "I will forward the information."

"Good, now what did you want?"

✝

"Hi, Reese, it's Kate."

"Hello, Kate, it's nice to hear from you."

"Reese, Rob's company usually gets three tables at the fund-raiser for the Children's Cancer Center. You know, the one on Hamilton Street?"

"Yes, I know the one you're talking about. The school has been trying to raise some funds for them as well," Reese said, sounding interested.

"Well, I know you are heading that effort at Roosevelt Elementary, and I wanted to invite you to be one of our guests at the fund-raiser the Bradleys are having this year. You, of course, can bring a date with you." Kate waited in anticipation.

"Oh, I think I would like that. Thank you, Kate. It's such a wonderful cause." Reese genuinely wanted to participate. She hesitated before she asked, "Kate, will Alex be there?"

Kate didn't want to lie but figured she could be creative with the truth. "Alex is swamped with work these days. I doubt that she will attend. But whether she does or doesn't I still would like you to come."

"Thank you, Kate. I would love to. When is it?"

"Next week, on the twelfth. Just let me know the name of your guest by Monday so I can put you both on the invitees list." Kate had a very broad smile on her face.

"Okay, I will let you know before Monday. Thanks, Kate."

"Sure, talk to you later, Reese, bye."

†

Kate hung up the phone and smiled to herself.

After all, it wasn't such a big lie. Alex is busy and I haven't heard technically if she is going yet, not really, Kate thought as she picked up her jacket and was off to speak with Vanessa Bradley. She was helping with the seating arrangements at the fund-raiser. This was going to be a night to remember. One way or another, Alex would either thank her or never speak to her again. Either way, she had to do something. She wasn't going to stand idly by and do nothing while Alex sunk lower and lower into the abyss.

†

November twelfth arrived. The fund-raiser was being held at the very prestigious Ranal's Country Club. The orchestra could be heard as guests left their cars to be valet parked and proceeded up the staircase, which would usher them to the grand ballroom.

There were approximately five hundred people attending. The Bradleys were well respected and the cause was near and dear to their hearts. The dinner was about to begin so all the guests were directed by their hostess to proceed to their assigned seats.

Kate and Rob arrived at their table first followed by a few other friends. Then Reese and her companion, Gail Ashby, arrived, with Alex and Elliot arriving last. Alex's and Reese's eyes met instantly. Both were frozen in time for a moment before Alex looked in Kate's direction, and her sister looked down. Alex was about to say something when Vanessa Bradley asked once more for everyone to be seated. Not waiting for Elliot, Alex pulled out her chair and sat down.

Both women avoided looking at one another. Alex wanted to leave—until she noticed Gail sitting next to Reese and decided she would not give them the satisfaction. If looks could kill, Gail Ashby would have died a million deaths.

The evening seemed to last forever and Reese looked more uncomfortable by the minute. Gail, looking quite smug, would lean over and whisper into Reese's ear. Alex looked furious. And Kate was rethinking her plan.

Rob leaned into Kate and whispered. "Sweetheart, what were you thinking?"

"I wasn't thinking," she answered.

Rob looked at her and smiled. "You are such a romantic, Kate. I don't know what I'd do without you." He pulled up her hand and kissed it.

Kate smiled and looked toward Alex who glared back at her, making her cringe. Reese still looked miserable. This was a total disaster.

When Vanessa started announcing the new sponsors, Alex's name was called and she was asked to rise. Reese looked at Alex as she started to sit down and their eyes met. For a moment, Alex's eyes were unguarded and Reese smiled but the connection only lasted a minute. After the announcements were all made, the party started and they all went their separate ways. Reese and Gail walked off in one direction, Alex walked in the other direction, and Kate and Rob just sat and breathed a sigh of relief.

Alex had left her cell phone on the table but didn't want to go back and get it fearing that she would have to face Reese again. So she walked over to the public phones to return some calls that were time sensitive on a case she was working on. When she finished, she bumped into Reese who was coming out of the ladies' room. Standing before one another neither could find anything to say until Reese spoke first.

"Alex, it was wonderful of you to become a sponsor," she said, giving Alex a genuine compliment.

Alex did not look away. "Thanks," she answered, unable to find any other words.

"Well, goodbye, Alex," Reese said sadly as she started to walk away.

Alex started to say goodbye when she remembered her anger and that was all that consumed her. "Where is your other half?" she asked in a voice filled with venom.

Reese, startled by the sudden change, became angry and turned around to face Alex. "Gail is my friend and not my *other half,* as you put it. In any case, Alex, it is none of your business!"

"Does she know that you're a love 'em and leave 'em kind of girl?" Alex asked insultingly.

Reese, unprepared for such an attack, didn't understand the meaning behind Alex's words. "Alex, this conversation is over!" She turned around to walk away but Alex grabbed her arm and pulled her into a secluded corner where she put Reese between the wall and herself.

"What would your *friend* say if she knew what a hypocrite you are? Or does she know already? Did you both laugh at me? Did you laugh at me when you were in bed with her?" Alex said through her teeth.

"Get out of my way, Alex."

"Did you laugh in bed with her about how you had made me love you? God, you disgust me," she said menacingly.

"I never laughed at you, Alex. I have never slept with Gail. Now get out of my way," Reese said as her eyes filled with tears and her anger began to build.

"I talked to her that day when you were in the shower. I know, Reese…I know you've slept with her," Alex finally yelled. "God, how I hate you!"

she growled. She pressed Reese closer to the wall until neither of them could breathe in air without the other one feeling it. And as before, Alexandra could not resist the desire to kiss those lips that had haunted her dreams night after night for the past months.

The kiss was passionate but not kind. For a moment, both women responded. Reese found in it the connection with Alex that she had missed but pulled away in indignation. Alex stood unable to move, as if the break had sapped her of all energy.

"Don't you ever kiss me like that again!" Reese exclaimed.

Alex's back was to her now.

Reese could not see the pain that covered Alex's face nor the tears rolling down her cheeks. "Stay away from me. I don't know what you are making yourself believe about Gail and me, and I don't care anymore, Alex. I have never slept with her! But if I ever do, it is none of your business. I don't know what's wrong with you, Alex. I just know that I can't and I won't deal with you ever again," she said as she walked away.

When Alex looked up again Gail was looking at Reese guiding her away. Gail looked at Alex and smiled. And at that moment, Alex realized she had been a fool—a first-class fool. It all became so clear as Alex stood there watching Gail guiding Reese through the crowd. *What have I done?*

Suddenly, Alex sprang into action and went after them but lost them in the crowd. Hurrying outside she scanned the parking lot. She had missed them. How could she have been so wrong?

Alex went inside, retrieved her things, and went out and got into a cab. The cabs had been there and available for those who chose not to drive after celebrating too much. All else was forgotten. Elliot would have to figure out she was gone and she would apologize later. She had to see Reese and talk to her. The only thought going through her mind on her cab ride to Reese's house was, *will would Reese ever forgive me.*

The cab pulled into the driveway and she paid the driver and got out. She assumed that the car parked in the driveway belonged to Gail, which made her walk faster, getting madder as she approached the front door.

She rang the bell. There was no answer so she rang it again and again.

When Reese pulled the door open, her mouth opened in surprise.

Alex stared at Reese's swollen lips thinking they looked like they had just been kissed. Reese had changed out of her clothes into slacks and a blouse. Had Gail helped her with that? Alex shook her head trying to remain focused as to why she was there.

Reese stood incredulous in front of Alex.

Chapter 8

"What do you want, Alex?" Reese asked, irritated.

"I want you. You are what I want, Reese. You said almost those very same words to me once." Alex looked down and then up to Reese's confused eyes. "I want you," she whispered.

"No."

"I made a mistake. It was all a mistake, Reese. I love you. Please let me talk to you so I can explain," begged Alex.

Reese was about to say something when Gail showed up behind her.

"What are you doing here? Haven't you hurt her enough already?" Gail stood next to Reese with her arm possessively around her shoulders. "You had your chance."

"Reese, I love you and you love me. Please let me talk to you. Please!"

"Alex..." Reese trailed off.

"What does it take to get rid of you?" Gail asked.

Furious, Alex directed her anger at Gail. "You! This is all your fault you lying—"

Reese interrupted her, visibly upset. "No, Alex, this is your fault. I don't know what you're trying to say, but I don't want any."

"I won't go," Alex said softly, not breaking eye contact with Reese. "Remember that morning? You said I was not alone. You said you would always love me. I need you, Reese. God, how I need you."

"Get out of here right now! She doesn't want you, get it?" Gail yelled.

"You just shut up! I'm not talking to you!" Alex yelled right back.

"Okay! Enough!" Reese yelled at both of them. "Both of you! Out!"

Both Alex and Gail stared at her. Gail went inside and got her things. As she walked by Reese, she said, "You're pitiful. I'm out of here."

"I am not leaving until I talk to you," Alex said again to Reese. "Please?"

"No! Go away," Reese said, trying to close the door. Alex put out her arm to stop the door from closing and quickly walked inside. "Alex, please leave."

"Reese, I need to talk to you. I promise I will leave if you want me to after I've said my piece, okay?" Reese looked at her and took a deep breath before she spoke again. "Alex, it took a long time to get used to the idea of not having you. It hurt to go to sleep at night and dream of you. I gave myself to you, Alex, like I never have to anyone before. I was there at every turn waiting for you, forgiving you, wanting you, loving you. I can't do it…I don't want to."

Alex stood frozen. What could she say to that? How could she fight the obvious truth of Reese's statements? She couldn't. For the first time since she arrived at Reese's door Alex looked defeated.

"You're right." She took a deep breath and ran her fingers through her hair in a tired gesture. "It was never you. It was always me. I was afraid. I could have believed in you as you…believed in me. It was easier to doubt and not take a chance."

"Alex, I don't understand." Reese walked further into the living room and sat down, covering her eyes.

Alex knelt down in front of her.

"I fell for the oldest trick in the book where Gail is concerned. But that's not the important thing. The important thing is that I should have trusted you. I have been telling myself that you betrayed me with Gail." Reese looked up and was about to speak but Alex rushed on. "I know you didn't betray me, Reese, you loved me. I know that. You see, we were becoming a family. You and Carly were becoming my family and I…" Tears started falling down her face.

Reese listened intently.

"I was afraid to love you both, to need you both. I have missed you and Carly so much, Reese. I was trying to spare myself the pain of losing you but this is worse…so much worse. You have a right to be angry with me. I know that you might not feel the same for me anymore, but please, please don't push me out of your life! Please," begged Alex as she dropped her head onto Reese's lap and cried, holding Reese tightly. "Don't hate me please, don't hate me. I couldn't bear it."

Reese caressed the dark hair in her lap. *How can one person be so confused,* she asked herself. Alex was so frightened of loving that she didn't allow herself to live. *Can I allow myself to be hurt again? Will Alex run away again?* These thoughts tormented her. She needed time.

"Alex, I don't hate you," she said gently.

Alex's tear-streaked face looked up before she reached out and pulled Reese into her embrace.

"Reese, please love me. Please, oh, God, please love me!"

Reese didn't have the heart to push her away.

Alex pulled back some and sought the lips that her soul needed to be able to heal.

The kiss was one of tenderness and love. Alex kissed her gently over and over again and all the while she kept whispering the only words she knew to be true. "I love you, Reese, I love you."

Reese sat on her sofa all night, holding Alex who had cried herself to sleep in her arms. She looked out the window and saw the first rays of the sun and then looked down at the woman in her arms. Her hand caressed the dark tresses of hair as she wondered what she should do.

When Alex left her life, she thought she would die. Reese had never experienced such pain. It had taken so much out of her not to fall to pieces in front of Carly as she did every night when she was alone in bed, wanting and crying for Alex. The dark, lonely nights were the worst. She had waited and loved Alex so much. She had given her all that she had held back from anyone before. And Alex had deserted her.

Reese was lost in thought and did not notice when Alex's eyes opened.

Alex saw the expression of anxiety then pain cross Reese's face and wondered if she was the reason. More likely than not, she was. Even after all that she had done, Reese had been there. Alex would never fail her again.

Reese looked down as she felt Alex's palm caress her cheek gently. When she looked into Alex's eyes, she was surprised to see the eyes that had taunted and tormented her all those long and lonely nights. She saw eyes filled with love, desire and the promise of passion beyond any she had ever known.

Reese closed her eyes, trying to shut out the memory.

"I will make it up to you a day at a time, love. Give me that chance. I will wait as long as it takes. Please give me that chance, Reese. I swear to you. Please look at me." Alex waited patiently until Reese looked into her eyes. "I won't fail you ever again. I will love that little blonde menace as if she was my own, and I will be by your side till my last day if you'll have me."

Reese got up from the sofa and walked to the window. Looking outside, she wrapped her arms protectively around her body. "Alex, I..."

Alex had followed her to the window and was a few feet behind her. She closed the distance between them quickly and held Reese close to her from behind. "You don't have to answer me now. You don't have to promise me anything. Day by day. Just give me the chance to show you, day by day." She felt Reese lean back against her body.

Reese closed her eyes. It would be so easy just to surrender. She needed Alex desperately. It would always be this way. Alex's words would have meant heaven to her a few months ago. Now, they were the words of promise for a tomorrow that she was afraid to hope for and then once again lose.

"I love you, Reese, I love you," Alex whispered in her ear.

Reese turned around in Alex's arms and pulled away.

"Rose will be dropping Carly off soon; Carly spent the night and I promised her I would make her a happy face pancake for breakfast this morning. I better go and get started."

Reese started to walk away when Alex reached out and pulled her into her embrace.

Almost immediately, Alex's lips covered Reese's. It had been so long since she had kissed her like this. All the need that had been stored away all those months came through the kiss.

Each woman pulled the other closer.

This they had always shared—their need to connect. All the resolve for patience was lost in the wave of desire that covered their bodies. Hands searched and caressed. Alex's lips went to the sides of Reese's face then down to her neck as Reese's head tilted back to allow passage.

The only thing that both bodies recognized was their need to be one. So much passion had been held back and it all threatened to boil over. Mouths hungered for skin and hands yearned to explore.

Suddenly, Reese felt Alex's mouth sucking on her breast. She looked down and could not remember how her blouse had opened. But a moan escaped her lips as she welcomed the waves of pleasure that followed.

The sound of the doorbell interrupted.

"Oh God, not again!" Reese exclaimed. "Alex, Alex, it's the door." She tried to put some order to the emotions that at that moment had been so thick that it restricted breathing. Alex held her for a moment without saying a word. Reese could hear her intake of breath as Alex tried to control it. She could feel the pounding of Alex's heart against her own chest. And when they started to pull apart, Reese saw eyes filled with love and passion-to-come looking back at her.

Both foreheads met lovingly; both took a deep breath before separating. Reese buttoned up her blouse and Alex tried to straighten her clothes. Reese walked unsteadily to open the front door.

The room was filled quite suddenly with a very energetic seven-year-old blonde dynamo. Who, as soon as she saw Alex, ran to her.

"Alex! Alex!" exclaimed Carly as she threw herself into Alex's arms.

Reese watched Carly in Alex's arms and her eyes filled with moisture at seeing Alex's face covered in tears as she held Carly tightly to her. She could see Alex whispering something into the little girl's ear and then Carly looked up at Alex, wiped Alex's tears away, kissed her cheek and hugged her tighter. Reese put her hand to her mouth to hold back her own tears from the emotions she was feeling at that moment.

Rose saw all this and stood in judgment. She knew all about Alex and how she had hurt Reese terribly. She was not about to get a free ride from Rose Hinckley. After Reese had confided in her that afternoon over coffee in her kitchen, Rose had become very protective of her friend. Over the last few weeks, Reese had become her dearest friend. Rose knew Reese to be a gentle and caring person. Now, putting a face to the person who had hurt her friend so badly, Rose's disapproval was clearly visible.

"Rose, it's all right," Reese said gently to her friend.

Rose looked from Alex to Reese.

"It's going to be all right, Rose." Reese's smile mixed with tears.

"Reese, are you sure?" Rose didn't hide her concern.

"Day by day, Rose. I'm going to take it day by day."

Reese watched Carly and Alex as they were now talking excitedly with one another. She saw Alex put the child down and, hand in hand, they walked into the kitchen. Reese looked back at Rose who had also been watching.

"Reese, please think about this before you get into a relationship with this woman again," said Rose.

"Rose, I love her." Reese smiled, putting her hand through her friend's arm. "Come on, have some breakfast with us. Meet Alex and give her a chance, Rose. You'll like her," she said as they both walked to the kitchen. "Where's Lindsey?"

"Dance class," Rose mumbled, "I don't want to like her," and Reese giggled as they both entered the kitchen.

Carly was sitting on a stool as Alex was leaning on the counter talking to her when Reese and Rose entered the kitchen. Alex looked up and smiled at Reese.

"Alex, this is my friend, Rose."

"Hi." Alex walked over and extended her hand to Rose. Rose hesitated before shaking Alex's hand.

Alex noticed the hesitation.

"Rose is going to be staying for breakfast," Reese said as she went to get out the pan to start on the pancakes.

"I'll make the coffee," Rose and Alex said at the same time. They both stood looking at one another until finally Rose broke the tension. "So, tall, dark, and good-looking, can you really make coffee?"

Reese burst out laughing and soon Rose and Alex joined in.

The ice seemed to have been broken.

"Well, that is just about the only thing I can do in a kitchen," Alex joked.

"Oh no, Alex, it's not. It's not," said Reese with a shy smile. Alex smiled tenderly in return.

Both women stared at one another for a moment with Rose looking on. She hoped that this time Alex would stay. She didn't want to like her but somehow it seemed right. The women belonged together.

As usual, Carly's playfulness broke the charged air in the room. "Alex, can we go stay with you this weekend?"

Alex looked at Carly and smiled. "We'll see, small fry." She smiled and went to caress the blonde head, putting a kiss on top of her head, before looking up at Reese.

"So, okay, who wants pancakes?" Reese asked.

†

The thought that Reese was back in her life kept going through Alex's mind as she drove into the office. For the last few days she had been visiting Reese and Carly as she had before. It was wonderful having them back in her life. Everything was so different now. She found that somehow her life had taken a new meaning. She would go over to Reese's house after she finished at the office and they would do something together, just as they used to. She would help put Carly to bed and then they would watch some television. They had kissed lightly, both anticipating but not wanting to push the other.

It mattered so much now to get it right. Alex didn't want to do anything to push Reese away from her. She would be patient and wait as long as she needed. Her thoughts were filled with a desire to make love to Reese just as she had so long ago. It became harder and harder with each passing day not to touch her.

Tonight, Alex decided, she would pick up a special dessert for after dinner. She knew Carly loved chocolate as much as she did so she would pass by the French bakery that she loved so much to pick up a chocolate mousse cake.

Alex tried to concentrate all morning on her paperwork, to no avail. Finally, she just gave up, leaned back in her chair, and let her thoughts loose. She closed her eyes and her mind filled with the bluest eyes taunting her. Her mouth opened slightly in anticipation of the mouth that she knew would bring her paradise.

"Ms. Masters, your sister is on line four," said Carol through the intercom. Alex shook her head in irritation.

"Okay, Carol, thank you."

"Hi, Kate," said Alex into the phone.

"Hello, Alex, how are you?" Kate asked cautiously. They had not spoken since the night of the fund-raiser.

"I am doing great. Sis, how are you?"

Kate was silent for a moment.

"Kate, you there?"

"Yes, I'm here. Everything is fine, huh?"

"Yes, Kate, everything is glorious!" Alex exclaimed.

"My God, you and Reese are back together again!" Kate yelled.

"How did you know?"

"Because you are happy, you idiot. God, Alex," she said happily. "I am so glad for both of you. How did it happen? When did it happen? What are your plans?"

"Whoa, whoa! One question at a time, okay?" Alex said happily.

†

"Mommy, are we going to stay with Alex this weekend?" Carly asked.

Reese looked at her daughter curiously. "Why do you like going to Alex's house so much munchkin?"

"Because, when we're there together she's not so sad about Teddy," Carly answered simply while she was eating her cookie. Reese looked at her and smiled as she reached out and caressed her daughter.

"Why do you think that, baby?"

"She told one time when she was tucking me in that when I was there she wasn't sad about Teddy anymore. She said I brought the sunshine back to her." Carly looked up at her mother. "Mommy, why did Teddy have to die? Was he sick?"

Touched by what Carly had revealed, Reese took a deep breath. "No, honey, Teddy was killed in a car accident. A man that had been drinking crashed into the car that he was in and he died." Reese looked at Carly to see her reaction.

"So, she never said goodbye to him?" her daughter asked.

"No, sweetheart, they never said goodbye."

"It's not fair, Mom."

"No, honey, it's not fair."

Both were silent for a little while. Carly covered her mother's hand and then hugged her before she looked at her mother again.

"You love her, don't you, Mom?"

Reese looked into those innocent eyes and answered truthfully. "Yes, baby, I love her very much," she said as her eyes filled with tears.

"Maybe if we both love her really hard she won't be sad anymore," Carly said as Reese took her into her arms and held her tightly.

"Yes, baby, we will love her so much that she won't be sad anymore."

As mother and daughter held each other, Alex walked into the kitchen.

"Hello, ladies."

Both Carly and Reese looked up.

Alex put down a box that said *La Bonne Bakery* and held a dozen red roses in her arms.

Reese smiled.

"This, small fry, is for you." She pointed to the box.

"What is it, Alex?" Carly asked excitedly.

"Chocolate mousse cake."

"Yummy!" Carly exclaimed as Alex walked over to Reese.

"And these are for you," she said as she gave Reese the roses. She leaned closer to kiss Reese then stopped as she looked at Carly peeking into the box and smiled.

Reese put her finger on Alex's chin, pulled her back, and proceeded to kiss Alex's lips lightly. "Thank you for the roses."

Alex smiled.

Chapter 9

It had been a whole month and Alex could not remember ever feeling this happy. After so much sadness and pain, she never thought that she would find happiness again. And yet, here she was driving to Reese's house and thinking how wonderful her life was right now. She would make Reese forgive her by showing her that she would wait. She would wait forever if she had to. But she would be there when Reese was ready.

Alex pulled into the driveway and as she got out of the car Carly came around the garage with a few little friends.

"Hi, Alex."

"Hi, small fry, who are your friends?" Alex asked with a smile.

"This is Ben," Carly pointed to a little boy with short blond hair on a green bicycle. "This is Patty."

Patty had brown hair that hung in two braids on the sides of her head.

"Nice to meet you guys," said Alex.

"Gonna go play at Ben's house…he just got a new jungle gym."

"Does mommy know?"

"Yep."

As the other two kids were waiting on their bikes, Alex looked around. "Hey, small fry, where's your bike?"

"It's broken," she said with a small pout.

"Oh, I see."

"Yeah…well, I'll see you later, okay?" Carly hugged her and followed her two friends to Ben's yard.

Alex watched her as she ran behind her two friends to the yard next door and saw them go in through the back fence before she proceeded to go inside. She walked into the house without announcing herself and was rewarded with a unique surprise. Reese was singing. Alex smiled as she followed the singing.

Alex poked her head into the laundry room as Reese was putting a load in the washer. *"I want to melt into you, I want your kisses to take me to paradise,"* Reese sang.

Alex came up behind her and pulled her to her. "I want that too," she said into Reese's ear.

Reese turned around quickly, scared to death. "Alex! You scared me!"

"Sorry love," Alex laughed.

Reese hit her in the arm with the palm of her hand. "You really scared me!"

"I'm sorry," Alex said softly.

Reese looked into the eyes that had always taken her breath away. As their gazes connected their mouths were pulled to their own connection.

Their bodies were barely touching. The kiss grew with passion, and Alex tasted the sweetness of the lips that she craved every moment of her day.

Reese stood still, not getting any closer, trying to capture the beauty of the moment. The fact that they were barely touching created more of a hunger between them. And inevitably, their passions collided to create a huge fire that hungered to be fed.

Finally, Alex's hands went around Reese's waist and pulled her closer.

Reese's arms went around Alex's neck, as her body seemed to melt into the warmth in front of her. Her fingers went into Alex's hair. She loved to feel Alex's hair. As her desire for Alex grew her fingers tightened around the dark tresses and she pulled Alex's mouth even closer to her.

Alex's hands slid down to Reese's bottom, pulling her closer as her mouth went down along her neck. She loved the taste of Reese's skin. The sounds coming from Reese's mouth only encouraged her to go further.

"Alex…Alex…how I've missed you," Reese said passionately. Alex's mouth went to meet her lips again. As they both gave in to the heat of their passion, Reese spoke the words that Alex had longed to hear. "Make love to me, Alex. Please make love to me."

†

An hour and a half later, Carly walked in to the kitchen and looked from Alex to Reese curiously.

"What's going on?" Carly asked.

"What do you mean, honey?" Reese asked her daughter.

"You two have goofy looks on your faces," Carly said, and both women broke out laughing. "What? I don't get it."

"Nothing, honey, really. We're making dinner," Reese said as the phone started to ring. She walked over to the phone and answered it.

"Hello?"

"Ms. Owens, this is Mrs. Perry. You wanted me to call you so we could schedule Carly's piano lessons."

"Oh, yes, Mrs. Perry, what time do you have available?" Reese asked excitedly. Alex and Carly listened attentively.

"I only have Thursdays at three thirty, I'm afraid."

"Oh, can I let you know tomorrow. I don't know if I can arrange it for that time." Reese sounded disappointed.

"All right, my dear. Let me know. Goodbye."

"Goodbye, Mrs. Perry." Reese hung up and stopped, considering her options.

"What's wrong, love?" Alex asked as she helped Carly up onto the stool.

"That was Mrs. Perry. She gives piano lessons and Carly wanted to take some," Reese answered, still distracted.

"What's the problem?" Alex asked.

"I don't think I can arrange it for Thursdays and Rose is just as busy."

"I'll take her," Alex said quickly with a smile.

Reese turned toward her in surprise. "Can you? Can you, Alex?"

"Of course, I'll just arrange it at the office. If I have any serious conflicts I'll let you know in advance, okay?" Alex finished with a smile.

"Great!" Reese kissed her lightly on the lips and smiled down at Carly.

"So, Alex is going to take me to my lessons?" Carly asked.

"Yep," Reese answered as she walked over to start dinner.

Alex leaned down and whispered in Carly's ear. "And if you try really hard we can have some chocolate ice cream on the way home, okay?"

"It's a deal," Carly said, shaking Alex's hand.

Reese gave them a questioning smile. "What are you two up to?"

"Us? Nothing," Alex answered as she and Carly exchanged a conspiratorial smile.

✝

Reese was getting her test papers from the right drawer of her desk when Rose entered the classroom.

"Hi there." Rose smiled as she walked up to Reese.

"Hello, Rose, I see you survived your brood today."

"Yes, the little darlings. I swear it's the same every year. Why is it the boys notice girls in fifth grade and they think the best way to get their attention is by putting gum in their hair?"

"Tough day, huh?" Reese sympathized.

"Not really. So how is it going with tall, dark, and gorgeous?" Rose asked as she sat down in a chair in front of Reese's desk.

"Oh, Rose, she is the most wonderful person..." Reese trailed off with a smile on her face.

"Yeah, yeah. I can see she has you wrapped around her finger." Rose smirked.

"Tell me you like her. Go on. You know you do!" Reese waited as she crossed her arms in front of her chest.

"Okay, I like her. I like her, okay!" Rose exclaimed in good humor. "Hey, where's Carly?" Rose asked, looking around the classroom. Carly usually waited in the classroom for Reese to finish her paperwork before going home.

"Alex took her to her piano lesson."

"So she's sticking, huh?" Rose asked warily.

"Yeah, she is." Reese smiled.

"I'm glad, you know," Rose said affectionately.

And Reese answered with a big grin. "Yeah, I know."

†

A few days later Reese and Carly pulled up to her driveway and found Alex was already there. As

183

Reese got out of the car, she noticed a huge empty cardboard box sitting next to the trash cans along the side of the house.

"What is she up to?" Reese asked out loud as she and Carly went up to the front door and walked in.

"Mommy, look!" Carly exclaimed as she ran to a beautiful red bicycle. It was the exact one she had wanted and they had talked about possibly getting. Reese just stood in shock.

Carly walked around it and then ran to Alex, hugging her before she ran back to her bike again. Alex's smile could not have been broader.

"You like it?" Alex asked excitedly.

"Yeah, it's perfect! See, this is the thingy that I was telling you about at the store that you go like this," she pulled at the bell, "and then like that."

Alex was totally lost in her fascination with the joy she had brought Carly. When she finally looked up, she saw Reese standing there with her arms crossed in front of her chest. Alex got up and walked up to her.

"I wanted to surprise her," she said meekly.

Reese uncrossed her arms and smiled. "Alex, it is a beautiful bike," Reese said patiently. She took her finger and lifted Alex's chin. "But, you just got her a PlayStation last week."

"But, Reese, it makes her happy." Alex took Reese into her arms with gusto.

"You are the pied piper. You know that?" Reese asked just before Alex kissed her.

†

"Hello, Kate," Alex said to her sister as the front door opened. Kate just stood aside as Alex waltzed in.

"Well, I finally get to see you. When are you guys coming over for dinner? Not planning on hibernating all winter are you?"

"I love you too, Kate."

"So, to what do I owe this honor?" Kate asked as she sat down.

Sitting down, Alex crossed her legs. "I need your opinion on something…"

Before Alex could finish Kate interrupted. "You? Need my opinion? Oh my God, the heavens and the tidal waves!" Kate exclaimed in humor.

"Okay, okay, very funny, but seriously. I want to give Reese a ring," Alex stated, looking for her sister's reaction.

"Alex, I think that's wonderful!" Kate said seriously. She knew what Alex was getting at. Alex was telling her that she was going to ask Reese to be a part of their family. Kate leaned forward and held her sister's hand. "She loves you Alex, and I know that she will make you very happy."

"Yeah, she does," Alex agreed as she blushed.

"Have you asked her?"

"No."

"Why not?" Kate asked concerned.

"I'm afraid she'll turn me down."

Kate was astonished. "Alex, she adores you, and Carly worships you!"

"I hurt her, Kate. I hurt her very badly. If she were to say no to me, I think I would die," Alex said very seriously.

Kate leaned in closer and put a stray lock of dark hair behind her sister's ear before she gently replied. "Alex, Reese loves you. Trust in that."

Alex looked up and Kate could see the fear in her green eyes. "I can't lose her, Kate."

Kate squeezed her hard. "You won't, sweetheart. You won't."

Alex smiled and her eyes looked hopeful.

"Now, let's go shopping!" Kate exclaimed.

†

Reese was stomping and raving. She was furious. "I can't believe you did this!"

"But—" Alex tried to say.

"No! No but's. I can't believe you went and did this without talking to me about it first!"

"Reese, if you only knew—"

"Alex, I am furious with you!" Reese yelled, stomping her foot again as Alex stood, chastised.

"Reese, try to understand…"

"Understand? Understand!"

"Okay, maybe that's not the right word." Alex tried to smile.

"Alex, I am not laughing and this is not funny. I can't believe you when out and bought a five- thousand-dollar piano for Carly and neglected to tell me!"

"But, Reese, she needed one and we passed by this store and she loved this one and..."

"And you bought it?" Reese stared at her, tapping her foot.

"Yes, it kind of worked out that way."

"Alex, you can't do this. We have to make these decisions together. That's what parents do. They consult one another. I mean, suppose she wants a car one day and I get home there's a new vehicle in the driveway? Alex, believe me you would be in for torture." Reese stopped talking as soon as she realized that Alex was staring at her strangely. "What is it?"

"You said that's what parents do," Alex repeated.

"Yes, and?" Reese confirmed, more confused than ever.

"You and me, Reese. You said yes! You finally said yes!" Alex shouted and took Reese into her arms. "You said yes!" she shouted. Reese looked at her and smiled as she shook her head. Alex put her finger under her chin and made her look into her eyes as those words rang through her heart. "You said yes," she repeated. They both stood looking into the eyes of love.

"Yes, Alex, yes," and as she finished saying the words Alex's mouth sealed their promise with a kiss.

Chapter 10

Alex had a smile on her face all day long. The changes that had taken place in her demeanor and character were so obvious that all the personnel at the law firm just stared when she passed by. Alex looked happy.

"Hello, Alex," Elliot said as he walked into her office and sat in the chair facing the front of her desk, prepared to get the truth about what was happening with her.

"Good morning, Elliot," Alex said cheerfully.

"Okay, so spill it."

"Spill what?" Alex asked in confusion.

"The smile on your face, the change in the last few weeks, everything."

"Elliot, I'm madly in love," Alex said happily.

"In love?"

"Yes."

Elliot got up, walked around the office and then sat back down again. "With who? Do I know him?" Elliot asked seriously.

"Yes, you know who it is."

"Who?" Elliot asked, waiting for the response.

"You've met her several times, Elliot," Alex said simply, waiting for Elliot's response.

He was silent, then got up again and paced around the office again before he sat back down. He looked at her and said nothing.

"I guess that's not the response I expected." Alex tried to hide her disappointment.

"Alex, I'm sorry. I just don't know what to say. It's the blonde, isn't it?"

"Her name is Reese Owens."

"She was at the fund-raiser with..." he trailed off.

"With somebody else," she finished for him.

"That's not what I meant…"

"Yes, it is. That's exactly what you meant." Alex got up, walked over to her window. With her back to Elliot she said, "I guess I expected you to be there for me even in this, Elliot. I have known you since college, you weren't just my partner in this law firm, I always saw you as my friend. You were my friend when I got married. You were my friend when I got divorced and you were my friend when I buried my son. I always thought you would be there like I was there when Mary left you."

"Alex..." Elliot began before falling silent. He remembered all those events in their lives. He especially remembered how supportive Alex had been when his wife of ten years just up and left him for someone else. Alex had been there to stop the gossip and put a gentle hand on his arm when the stress that followed filled his life. Ashamed, he asked himself why could he not support her in this.

When Elliot said nothing more, Alex turned around and did not look at him as she sat down at her desk and started going through papers. "Well, that's that. I really am busy, Elliot."

He got up but before he walked out, he looked in her direction again. "I'm sorry, Alex."

She looked up. "I am too, Elliot." She quickly went back to her paperwork. When she heard the door close, she looked up again at the door and her eyes misted over. "I'm sorry too, Elliot." Alex whispered sadly.

†

"Reese, I'm glad for you. She is a very, very lucky lady," Rose said as she gave her friend a hug.

"Oh, Rose, she is everything I want and need. I have never felt anything for anyone close to what I feel for Alex," Reese confided in her friend.

"I can tell. Your face lights up when she enters a room, kiddo."

Reese smiled. "Yeah."

"Well, what are you guys planning and all that stuff?"

"What do you mean?"

"Well, this means that you change things," Rose said to a very confused Reese. "You know, Reese, you say yes and then *dadum*!"

"What is *dadum*?"

"Well, it usually means, you know, living together, inviting friends over for dinner, sharing a life, getting old, having grandchildren. But I think you start by living in the same house," Rose finished with a chuckle.

Reese sat down stunned. "My God!"

"Yeah, it's the big step, babe."

At that same moment, Alex burst into the living room. Both Alex and Reese stared at each other.

Rose smiled. "I guess it hit you too, huh?" she said comically to the two lovers who were just standing there, looking at each other in shock.

Alex looked at Rose and acknowledged Rose's question with a nod then walked over to Reese. "I want to live with you yesterday," Alex said simply.

Reese smiled and nodded as well. "Okay."

"Your place or mine?" Alex asked as they got closer and closer to one another, oblivious of their friend now.

"Wherever you want."

"Whatever makes you happy," Alex replied, taking a step closer.

"You make me happy."

"I love you," Alex said, closing the distance and taking Reese in her arms for a kiss.

"Well, you both love each other, but you still haven't figured out where to live yet," Rose said mostly to herself. Rose smiled and sat down, shaking her head. "I gotta tell you guys, you're gonna have to talk more than this to plan a move." Rose kept talking as the two continued kissing, oblivious to anyone but each other.

†

"Alexandra, what are your plans?" Kate asked with irritation.

"What is it with everybody? Rose is on the same wavelength. Have you met Rose? Are you two clones or what?" Alex joked.

"Seriously, Alex, what plans have you two made?"

"We haven't really made any concrete plans. I thought maybe a nice romantic dinner for two and we could discuss all the details," Alex said with a smile.

"Sounds perfect."

"Can you babysit Carly?"

"Absolutely, she is a darling little thing, and Kevin loves to play with her. When?"

"Is tonight too soon?"

"Nope, perfect."

"Great, thanks, Kate." Alex kissed her sister and started toward the door.

"Alex?"

Alex turned to face her sister. "Yeah?"

"What about Mom and Dad?" Kate looked seriously at Alex.

"They will never understand, Kate, you know that."

"I know. But, Alex, you have to tell them. Does Reese know what to expect with Mom and Dad?"

"No, we haven't really discussed her parents or mine." Alex sat down.

"Maybe you should," Kate suggested gently.

"What will I say to her? That they'd rather have me miserable and still be their perfect daughter than happy with her?" Alex said sarcastically.

"Alex, you can tell her the truth and prepare her. She has a right to know." Kate stepped next to her sister and put her hand lovingly on her shoulder. "Thanksgiving is just around the corner."

Alex looked up. "Oh God, I forgot about that."

"She will love you no matter what. Build this relationship on a strong foundation, Alex. That way it will always be strong even with Mom and Dad."

"I don't know if anyone can survive Mom and Dad." Alex could not hide her concern at the prospect of Reese meeting her parents.'

"Reese is stronger than you think."

"How did you get so smart?" Alex asked her sister lovingly.

"Always been this way," Kate answered with a smile.

"You are the best, Kate. The best... love you, you know." Alex embraced her sister.

Kate was at first taken by surprise but then her arms went around Alex as well. "I love you too, stinky."

Alex pulled away with a smile on her face. "Hey, you haven't called me *stinky* in years."

"You haven't been around in years," Kate answered and hugged her sister again as she whispered, "Welcome back, Alexandra, I missed you."

†

"I've met someone I love very much and who loves me," Reese said. There was silence on the other end of the telephone. "Dad?"

"Yes, I'm here. Do we know her?" Donald Owens asked apprehensively.

"No, you don't know *her,* Dad," Reese said and was greeted again by silence from her father.

"Well, I'm glad that you are happy, Reese."

"Are you, Daddy?" Reese asked, unable to control the sob that escaped her.

"Yes, baby, I am. I know that I don't always know what to say to you, but I am glad that you are happy."

"Thanks, Dad. I wish you could meet her. She is so wonderful. Carly adores her and she loves me. She really and truly loves me." Reese stopped to take in a breath.

"I'm glad, Reese. I'll talk to Mom about her. You know she'll be difficult about it, but she will come around. She always does. Well, I love you, baby."

"I love you too, Daddy, bye." Reese hung up the telephone and stood for a moment in deep thought. They were wonderful people, her parents—

loving and understanding as she and her sister Patricia had grown up. They had been so proud when she went to college and so disappointed when she had told them she was gay. Nothing had been the same after that. The pain of what she saw in her parents' eyes still hurt.

Somehow, the fact that she was gay erased all else that had preceded their knowing. Reese had to admit that she had expected a different reaction from them. She knew that, in some ways, they had cut some of the ties to her. Patricia, her sister, had dropped out of school and run off with a boy only to come back pregnant and alone. Reese had been there to support her and help her, making them closer to each other.

After a year, Patricia did meet a nice young man, as her dad had put it, and settled down. Mark had been a good father to her nephew Christopher, and they now had two more children, Donny and Amanda.

As the years passed by, her parents never had time to come and see her and Carly because they had gotten so involved with Patricia and their other grandchildren, and Reese had felt the slight more than once. Why did she care? *Because I just do* was the answer she always gave herself.

She was suddenly surrounded by a warm body and pulled into a loving embrace.

"Hello, lady," a soft voice said into Reese's ear.

"Hello, stranger. I didn't even hear you come in." Reese leaned back into the comforting hold.

"You seemed miles away."

"I was," Reese said softly.

Alex turned her around and pulled her to her again. Concerned, she asked, "Are you all right, love?"

"I am now," Reese said as she went deeper into Alex's arms.

Alex held her tighter. "What happened?"

"I told my father about us."

"Oh? And what did he say?"

"He's glad that I'm happy, and that you are so wonderful, and that Carly is so happy…"

Reese broke into tears and Alex pulled her closer and stroked her hair. "It's all right, sweetness," she whispered into Reese's hair. "It will be all right."

"Alex, why can't they just be glad that we're happy?" Reese asked, now looking into Alex's eyes.

"I don't know, Reese. I don't know."

†

"Hello, Mother," Alex said politely.

"Alexandra, what a wonderful surprise. How are you, dear?" Vanessa Masters asked her daughter.

"Very well, thank you."

"How is your sister? I haven't heard from her and have left several messages on that answering machine of hers."

"Katherine is fine."

"Good, tell her to call me. We plan to arrive a few days before Thanksgiving."

"I will pass that message to her, Mother."

"Now, why are you calling me, Alexandra? I know it must be important."

"Mother, I have met someone who makes me very happy and that I have fallen in love with,"

Alex said, getting it off her chest before taking a deep breath.

"Alexandra, that's wonderful. I am so happy for you, my dear. Do we know him? What is his name? I hope we get to meet him for Thanksgiving." Vanessa Masters asked in genuine interest.

"Her name is Reese, and no, you don't know her but I hope you get to meet her at Thanksgiving," Alex said simply. The silence lasted a lifetime.

Finally, Vanessa Masters carefully spoke. "I must have misunderstood what you said, Alexandra, I thought—"

Alex cut her off, "No, Mother, you didn't."

"Have you lost your mind," Vanessa stated in a matter-of-fact tone.

"Is that what you want to think? That I'm crazy? Would that make it okay, Mother? Would you rather I were crazy than happy?" Alex yelled into the telephone.

"Don't raise your voice with me, Alexandra! What have you been doing? I knew you were not well, but I didn't realize that you had lost your hold on reality too," exclaimed Vanessa Masters. "You are obviously not well, Alexandra!"

Neither mother nor daughter wanted to relent or give the other a foothold so the silence grew heavy between them.

Finally, Alex took a deep breath and spoke, her voice filled with pain and a note of weariness. "Mother, I have found someone to love who loves me. For the first time in years, I wake up and don't want to die. You can't imagine what it's like to want to die every time you open your eyes. I wake up now and am hopeful that the day will not be full of memories that fill me with pain. She gives me joy, Mother. She makes the pain inside me bearable. Be happy for me. Can't you be happy for me?" Alex finished softly, almost in a plea.

"I can't discuss this with you now, Alexandra…I can't."

As the telephone line went dead, Alex held the telephone against her ear until the buzzing shook her out of her trance. She replaced the receiver in its cradle as the tears rolled down her cheeks.

Chapter 11

"Alex!" Carly called out.

"Hey, small fry." She opened her arms and they were immediately filled with a very energetic little blonde person. "Where's mom?"

"Inside. Are we going somewhere today?"

"Yes, we're going to the Bronx Zoo."

"The what zoo?"

"The Bronx Zoo, it's a wonderful place. You're going to love it." Alex started to tickle the child's tummy.

"Stop!" yelled Carly in laughter.

"Now take me to your leader or the tickle monster will attack," Alex said in a low voice. She put Carly down and chased her into the house.

"Mom, Mom," Carly yelled as she ran through the door chased by the tickle monster.

"Whoa, what is going on?" Reese asked as she entered the living room.

Alex immediately took Reese into her arms. "Tickle monster needed to be fed."

"Oh really?" Reese smiled from her daughter to Alex.

"Yes," Carly said very seriously.

"Oh, well, proceed then." Reese stepped out of Alex's embrace. Carly squealed as Alex chased after her, leaving Reese laughing.

✝

"You think she had a nice day at the zoo?" Alex asked softly as she and Reese put a sleeping Carly to bed.

"I think she had a blast."

"Here, I'll put those in the hamper in her bathroom." Alex grabbed the clothes that Carly had worn to the zoo.

"Okay, I'll finish putting on the pajamas."

Alex stopped and smiled.

Reese smiled back before Alex turned around and left the room.

An hour later, they sat in the living room finally making plans about their future.

"We should talk to her, don't you think?" Alex said with concern in her voice.

"Yes, we will talk to her tomorrow," Reese said as she moved closer to Alex.

"I mean, I want her to be happy with all this."

"She will be happy. She loves you," Reese said, getting even closer.

"I want her to, you know, look at me someday like I…I don't know," Alex mumbled.

"Like her mother," Reese said, finishing the sentence for her.

Alex looked up into loving eyes and answered, "Yes, like I'm her mother."

"Oh, love, she looks at you that way already," Reese said as she ran her fingers through Alex's hair and was rewarded with a sweet smile.

"You think so?"

"I know so."

"I love you, Reese Allison Owens."

Reese gave her a big smile before she asked, "Who told you my middle name?"

"Our daughter," Alex said before her mouth sought its mate.

"Alex…I don't want you to go," Reese said huskily.

Alex's mouth found Reese's. It never stopped surprising her how in one moment, with a mere word from the woman in her arms, her body became filled with desire. She had wanted Reese all day. Her hands worked open the buttons on Reese's blouse then reached in and cupped the breasts that she sought with desperation.

Reese gasped, her senses overwhelmed by the need Alex produced in her. From the very first moment they met, Alex had been able to reduce her defenses to nothing. Reese surrendered to the passion every time Alex touched her. Matching Alex's desperation her hands pulled at Alex's slacks.

Their passion overrode any sense of waiting. Mouths tasted and hands touched. Moans of pleasure and of need filled the space of their world. They fused with such want that all else dissipated as they reached the peak of their passion simultaneously. Finally, sleep claimed them and they fell asleep in each other's embrace.

†

The light coming through the window awakened Alex. She felt the body of the woman she loved partially on her and kissed the blonde hair smiling as she held Reese closer. Still half asleep, she looked around at her surroundings and then her eyes flew open. They had fallen asleep on the sofa, and they were both naked. Her eyes got even wider when she heard Carly coming down the stairs. She grabbed a shawl from the back of the sofa and tried covering them as much as possible.

Reese just got closer and held on tighter to her lover.

"Reese…Reese, Carly is coming down the stairs," Alex whispered.

"That's nice, sweetheart," Reese mumbled, half asleep.

"Reese, sweetheart, you and I are naked," Alex said into her ear.

Reese's eyes flew open.

"Good morning, guys," Carly said as she sat on the chair across from the two partially covered women lying together on the sofa. "Can we go to McDonald's for breakfast?"

Both women nodded their heads in affirmation.

"Mom, can I go over to Ben's house? He called and invited me to come over today. I forgot to ask you," Carly finished saying with a yawn.

"Sure, honey, we'll talk about it, okay? Why don't you go and get dressed so we can have breakfast," Reese encouraged.

"Okay," Carly said as she walked up the stairs.

Reese and Alex stared at one another and smiled. "I guess that takes care of one conversation," Alex said.

"Carly knows about me, Alex. I have always been honest with her. I will confess that I spoke to her about us."

"You did?"

"Well, not exactly, but I did tell her that I love you and she understands that you love me and we love her, so she is okay, because she is happy and secure with our love for her. I just didn't expect to test it like this that's all," Reese said with a smile.

"Reese, I want this to work. I need this to work. I was worried that she wouldn't understand."

"You worry too much, you know that?"
"You have mentioned that before."
"We better get dressed."
"Yes, I can only take one heart attack a day," Alex said in relief.

✝

Alex and Reese agreed that only Carly and Alex should go to McDonald's for breakfast. Reese was sure about how Carly felt about them but she realized that Alex needed to have the conversation with Carly in order for Alex to put her doubts to rest. Only Carly could take those doubts from her. Reese was touched at Alex's concern for Carly's feelings.

✝

"How is that hash brown?" Alex asked.
"Yummy! I wish we could have McDonald's all the time."

210

"Well, if we did, maybe it wouldn't be so special would it?"

"Maybe," Carly said after a pause.

"Hey, kiddo, I wanted to talk to you."

"Okay, what about?"

Uncomfortable, Alex said, "About your mom and me."

"Are you going away again?" Carly asked visibly upset.

"No…no, I want to live with both of you forever and ever," Alex said quickly.

"You do?"

"Yeah, I want to make sure that it's okay with you." Alex waited anxiously.

"You mean you would be like a second mom and all that?" Carly asked.

"I would like to be if you let me." Alex waited nervously.

"Yeah, I would like that, Alex," Carly replied with a smile.

"I love you to infinity and back again you know," Alex said as her eyes filled with tears.

"Yeah, I know." Carly smiled and put her small hand over Alex's bigger one.

"You know, I love your mom very much," Alex said, preparing herself for the latter part of her speech.

"I know," Carly agreed as she started munching on her hash brown again.

Alex took a long breath and continued. "Carly, when two people love each other like your mom and I do, they...well, they want to build a life together. They want to plan a future and build it so that it will last. And in order to do that, it must be built on honesty and love." Alex looked at Carly who stared at her in confusion. "Okay, let me try again. When two people love each other like your mom and I do..."

"Alex?"

"Yes, sweetheart?"

"You and Mom and me should all live together, right?"

"Yes, I would like that very much," Alex answered in astonishment.

"Where will we live? At your house or ours?" Carly asked as she started to chew on her hash brown again.

"Umm…well, that is a very good question. I thought maybe we should all look for a new house together. You know, like something for all of us to choose as a family. What do you think about that?" Alex asked.

"Yeah, I guess."

"You don't like the idea?"

"Can it have a pool like your house?"

"Absolutely," Alex said with a big smile.

"Okay, that's a plan then."

"Well, I think we better talk to your mom about it don't you?"

"Yeah," Carly returned the smile.

Chapter 12

"Katherine! What is going on over there?"

Kate pulled the phone away from her ear. "Hello, Mother."

"Katherine, have you talked to your sister lately?"

"Mother, I know all about Reese and Alex." Kate prepared herself for the verbal onslaught from her uptight mother.

"Katherine, why didn't you call us? She needs to see a psychiatrist. I didn't realize that she had gotten worse. Dear Lord, if people find out her reputation will be ruined."

"Mother, how could you say such a thing? Alexandra has thought about nothing but others all her life. She was the good daughter…the perfection you and Daddy wanted her to be. This time it's her turn, Mother. Don't ruin it for her. She loves Reese; she needs her. Alex has come back to us, Mother. If you could only see how happy she is now," Kate said, trying to persuade her mother.

"Katherine Anne, you surprise me. You have known about this for a while haven't you?" Vanessa asked in indignation.

"Mother, you haven't heard a word I've said. Alex is no longer suicidal! Do you understand it now? I honestly thought that one day I would get the call that she was dead." Kate only heard silence so she continued. "You didn't want to see it; neither did Daddy. Would it be better if she had died, Mom? My sister is alive and actually looking forward to living. Remember that next time you talk to her."

"Katherine, you know I love, Alexandra," Vanessa said softly.

"Maybe you should let her know it."

"I don't think I can handle this situation with Alexandra," Vanessa said honestly.

"I'm sorry to hear that, Mother. I will be here for her. I love her as she is now more than how she was before she met Reese."

After a long silence, Vanessa abruptly ended the conversation. "I will talk to you later, Katherine, love to Rob and Kevin. We will see you all for Thanksgiving."

Kate hung up the phone and a sigh. This would hurt Alex terribly. Thanksgiving was going to be a real trial.

"God, I hope Alex is strong enough for this," Kate said sadly to herself.

†

"Hello, you two," Reese welcomed Alex and Carly into the house after their breakfast trip to McDonald's.

"Hi, Mom. Alex and I have something that we would like to talk to you about," Carly said excitedly.

"You do, huh?"

"Yes, we have some family decisions to make," Carly said with a grin. Reese looked at Alex and her reward—a huge smile.

†

"Well, that is making progress. You two are going to start looking for a house soon?" Rose asked.

"This weekend. We called a realtor and listed both houses. Dealing with two moves is going to be hazardous to all our health. We have to get rid of tons of junk and then somehow mix what we both have. I don't know…it may be better just to start from scratch.

"I do know this is going to be really hard on Alex," Reese said sadly.

"Yeah, she's going to have to dismantle Teddy's room," Rose agreed.

"Rose, this is going to be really hard. You didn't see her that night. She fell to pieces. I don't know how she is going to take doing this." Reese's voice was filled with her concern.

"Like she said to you before, a day at a time. She has you now. She didn't have that before. Reese, you make her happy, and from what I have heard, that is something she hasn't been in a long time." Rose tried to reassure her friend.

"Rose, she comes across as so strong and unapproachable sometimes to people. I have seen her just cut somebody up with her words both in her office and out of it. They all think she is made of stone. She's not like that, Rose. She is so frail inside. If you touch her wounds she falls to pieces; I think in some ways it is only now that she is dealing with losing Teddy. God, that night I thought her pain would kill her. I'm afraid, Rose, I'm afraid," Reese finished as her eyes started spilling over with tears. Rose took in her into her arms.

†

Alex had taken to staying at Reese's house during the week. This way she was there to tuck in Carly and help get her ready for school. Loving Reese had made her feel alive again. Loving Carly had helped fill some of the emptiness that losing Teddy had left in her.

One afternoon, she had gone to pick up something at the store and quite suddenly turned toward her house. Alex walked in and looked around. This had been her home, one she shared with Teddy. She had taught him to swim in the pool. She remembered how many times he had come down those

218

stairs. And in her memory, she became lost in her past...

"Mommy! Mommy! Come on." Teddy ran out and jumped in the pool. Alex had splashed in right behind him.

"I got you!" Alex exclaimed as she picked him up as they played in the water.

"Teach me how to swim underwater, Mom."

"Okay, I'll tell you what, when Daddy drops you off tomorrow, we will go get a snorkel and fins and then we can start practicing next weekend. Okay?"

"Oh, Mom, why can't we do it now?"

"'Cause we are in the pool, wet and all, you silly monkey," Alex said as she tickled Teddy until he squealed.

Later that night, James had picked him up. She kissed Teddy and tousled his hair. As they drove away, she could see him turn and wave goodbye to her through the back window. She remembered waving back. Later that night she figured she would surprise him so she went to buy the snorkel and fins at the sports store. She would have them gift-wrapped.

Alex walked to the hall closet and took out the gift-wrapped boxes. She held them to her and leaned against the wall, sliding down to the floor. Her anguish echoed throughout the empty house. The tears kept coming as she continued to hold onto the packages for a very long time.

She relived that last day with Teddy over and over again. She was lost in her memories, lost in her pain. Hours later, when Reese found Alex she knelt down in front of her and reached a hand out to caress Alex's face. Alex couldn't speak and the tears came again. She clutched the boxes to her again and looked down at them.

Reese looked down as well before pulling Alex gently into her embrace. "I love you, Alex, I love you," she whispered into Alex's ear.

Alex reached out for her as the sobbing shook her body. Reese held on tightly.

"He's gone. I promised I would teach him to snorkel. See?" Alex pulled away long enough to show Reese the boxes that were now crushed to her.

"Reese, it hurts. It hurts so much," Alex said as she went once again into the only arms that gave her any comfort.

Reese cried with her and held her tightly. After a long time Alex looked into the eyes of her lover. Because that is what Reese was to her. Reese was love; love had finally come to save her.

Reese caressed Alex's face. "We can live here if you want, Alex. I want you to be happy."

Alex smiled weakly. "No, we have a life to build you and I. Carly deserves a home. This was Teddy's home, not Carly's. Teddy will be with me forever. Carly deserves her own time and space."

"Alex, I love you more than my heart can bear sometimes." Reese's tear-filled eyes expressed so much love. "My daughter is blessed to have you in her life."

Reese leaned over and kissed Alex's mouth lightly. They both got up and Reese held Alex as they walked to the front door. Pausing for a moment, Alex put the crushed boxes on a coffee table. As they walked outside, she turned around and looked back once more before shutting the door. This had been her time with Teddy. She knew she had to let this house go so that she could build a life with Reese and Carly. After all, her memories would always be with her. She had the laughter and the joy that Teddy had given her. Reese had given her that back. Reese made her remember the joy. Alex said her good-byes and they walked away.

†

"How did you know where to find me?" Alex asked as she went further into Reese's embrace. They were in bed after having picked Carly up from Kate's house and putting her to bed.

"I got worried when you didn't come back. I dropped Carly off at Kate's and knew I would find you at the house," Reese said as she kissed the top of Alex's head.

"I love you, you know," Alex whispered.

"I love you too, darling."

"Are you okay?"

"I will be. I will be." Alex held Reese tightly and felt the tightening of Reese's arms around her. *Yes, I will be all right. I will be all right.*

†

"You have got to be kidding?" Alex asked looking at Kate.

"No."

"They are coming for Thanksgiving?"

"Yep, that's what she said."

"Oh no, Kate, this is not good." Alex started to pace in Kate's kitchen.

Kate kept on making a pie.

"Why? Why are they coming?"

"Why does Mother do anything?"

Alex stopped and looked straight at her sister. "Why are you so okay with this?"

"Alex, I have learned to deal with Mother's bigger-than-life decisions. You know as well as I do that it makes no difference what you and I say…*she is coming*."

"Yes, I know."

"Alex?" Kate stopped what she was doing and Alex looked at her. "Do you love Reese?"

"What kind of question is that?"

"It's a sincere question. Do you love her?"

"This is ridiculous." Alex's arms went up in the air as she started walking out of the kitchen.

"Love is staying, Alex, not running away," Kate said harshly.

Alex turned around and faced Kate. "What are you talking about?"

"Answer my question. Do you love Reese?"

"You know I do."

"Say it."

Alex just stood and stared at Kate.

"It's scary, Alex. But remember how she makes you feel. If it's real, the words are easy." Alex looked down and when she looked up again, Kate could see the raw emotion in her eyes.

"I love her more than I can bear sometimes," Alex said honestly. "I don't want Mother to scare her off. I couldn't bear losing her. I wouldn't know how to live without her. I'm afraid, Kate."

Kate walked over to Alex and took her in her arms. "You've been dealing with a lot lately. It's called living again."

Alex pulled away and Kate smiled.

"Alex?" Kate called out.

"Yes?" Alex waited with her back to her sister.

"Reese loves you more than you know. Nothing will make her leave. Only you can do that."

"Thanks, Kate," Alex sincerely said as she left.

Kate had a wide smile on her face. She felt good. Alex was going to be okay.

†

"The realtor called me today. She says there's a house that is perfect for us. I stopped by to see Kate…my mother and father are coming for Thanksgiving. Oh, and the realtor says that it has a beautiful pool. Remember how funny it was when Carly started telling her…"

Reese interrupted.

"Wait, wait. Your parents are coming for Thanksgiving?" Reese asked, waiting for an answer.

"Couldn't get it past you, huh?"

"Nope, spill the beans, counselor."

Alex walked over to Reese with a very serious look on her face.

"I called my mother a few weeks ago and told her about us. My mother suggested I see a shrink. I should have told you. I'm sorry," said Alex, not knowing what reaction she would get from Reese.

Reese walked toward the window and looked out without saying anything.

Alex waited where she stood.

"Yes, Alex, you should have told me. I told you about calling my father."

"Reese, I'm sorry."

"I know you are." Reese turned around and faced her now. "You have to include me in your life. That means everything. Remember, Alex, it's for better or for worse."

Alex closed the distance between them. She stood close enough to Reese to touch her and yet she didn't.

"I knew it would upset you. My mother is...well difficult," Alex said dryly.

"Do you think it was easy to tell my father? I knew what he was going to say. It's the same line all the time. *Glad to know that you are okay but oh...you are still our gay daughter.* It hurts, Alex. But I wanted them to know that you exist for me. I keep hoping that someday they will understand. But I shared it with you." Reese was now very emotional. "When will you accept that you are not alone anymore? Your pain and your happiness are mine too?"

That's all Alex needed to hear. She took Reese into her arms and held her tightly. "I'm sorry, love. I don't know what I did to deserve you. I thank God you came into my life each and every day. Don't give up on me, Reese. Don't give up on me, please?"

"Alex, sometimes you are really stupid." Reese said as she pulled away and looked into Alex's eyes. "I love you. Get used to it. I am not going anywhere. Nothing, do you hear, nothing or no one is going to take me away from you."

"Did you just call me *stupid*?" Alex asked, amused.

"Well...I'm sorry, darling. But sometimes you do drive me crazy!" Reese smiled.

"You called me *stupid*," Alex said with a pout.

"Oh, don't be like that my little stupid girl," Reese said in baby talk.

"Now, I am really insulted!" Alex pouted, crossed her arms and turned her back to Reese.

Reese came up behind her and pressed herself into Alex's back. "What can I do to make it up to you, love," Reese whispered into Alex's ear.

Alex's arms came down to her sides and pulled Reese behind her even closer as she leaned back. "I can only think of one way."

"Oh?"

Alex turned around and saw the same passion she felt in her in Reese's eyes. Alex's hand caressed the face she loved as her lips brushed across Reese's jaw, her teeth nibbling lightly along Reese's neck.

A moan escaped Reese's mouth as her hands pulled Alex closer to her.

Alex's hands found their way inside Reese's blouse. Reese's nipples were already hard with the anticipation of the touch. Reese pulled Alex closer to her and started kissing Alex's neck lower and lower.

"Carly?" Alex asked in a groan.

"Girl Scouts."

"I love Girl Scouts."

"Alex, stop talking and make love to me."

"Yes, ma'am."

Chapter 13

"Come in, Elliot." Alex waved Elliot into her office.

"I know that you're busy, but I need to go over these files with you."

"Sure, what's up?"

"Alex, Brian Stravinsky is suing LNSG for breach of contract."

"You're kidding. And they want us to handle it?"

"They want you to handle it," Elliot said smugly.

"Elliot...this is *big*. I mean really *big*."

"I know. If you pull this off, Alex, we're talking senior partnership."

"It couldn't have happened to a better person," she said jokingly.

Elliot laughed as well.

"Give those files to me. I'm dying to start my notes. Have we got all the paperwork from Stravinsky yet?"

"Slow down," Elliot said, still laughing. "How about if we go and celebrate?"

"Sounds great, I can't believe this. Wow. Oh, and I will want a golden parachute clause along with that partnership."

"Absolutely," Elliot said with a smile. "You've worked hard for this, Alex, congratulations." Elliot got up and went to Alex. He pulled her up from her chair and took her in his arms, giving her a warm hug.

"Thank you, Elliot, thank you," she said with a smile as she pulled away.

Elliot leaned in and kissed her. When she pulled away, he held on still.

"Let me go," she said seriously. Gone was the friendly banter between them.

"Give me a chance, Alex?" Elliot asked, still holding her tightly.

"Let me go now!"

Elliot released her.

"I am with someone, Elliot."

"You are with a woman, Alex. It's a phase. It'll pass."

"You are delusional," she blurted out at him.

"Alex, you and I have things in common. I know I can make you happy. I have been waiting for you to come out of your self-imposed mourning for these past two years," Elliot finished.

Alex stared at him as if she were seeing him for the first time. "I thought we were friends, Elliot. I'm sorry you thought anything else. I am involved…I told you that weeks ago. If you've chosen not to recognize that involvement, that's your problem not mine," Alex said, leaving no grounds for argument.

Elliot, however, would not give up that easily. "She can't possibly satisfy you, Alex."

"Why you pompous ass! I love her, I want her and she satisfies me in every way, Elliot."

"I don't believe you."

"You don't have to!" she yelled back.

"Alex, she's beautiful but…"

"Elliot, this conversation is over, Now get out!" she said as she pointed to her door.

"Alex, we have known each other a long time…"

"Elliot, there is nothing left to say between us. What part of that don't you understand?"

Elliot walked toward the door and before he reached it, he turned around to face Alex yet again. "She will never be able to share what we have between us."

"I share everything with her already, Elliot. There is nothing I haven't shared with her. She has my dreams, my hopes, my future, and my passion, Elliot. She has everything."

Elliot stared at her in disbelief, then turned around and walked out of her office. Alex had accepted that her relationship with Reese would end some connections she had with friends, family, and the world she lived in. But, Reese was her life and she would gladly give it all up for the happiness that she now felt inside.

†

"Carly, will you get that for me, honey?" Alex called out.

"Okay, Alex. Hello?" Carly answered the telephone. "Who is this?" asked a censorious woman's voice.

"This is Carly. Who are you?"

"I am Vanessa Masters. Who are you?"

"I am…I'm Alex's daughter," Carly said finally. Yes, that was what she was now that Alex and her mom had explained it all to her.

"Who?"

"You know, I'm Carly," said the girl innocently.

"I know your name. What do you mean you are Alexandra's daughter?"

"'Cause I am. She's my mom now too."

Alex walked into the room carrying a big box. "Who is it, honey?"

"Who should I say is calling?" Carly asked.

"Tell her it's her mother."

"Okay, wait okay?"

"Fine."

Carly gave Alex the telephone. "She says she's your mother." Alex looked at Carly and immediately took the telephone from her.

"You okay, small fry?" Alex searched the child's face.

"Yep, can I go outside Alex?"

"No, honey. I don't want you outside near the pool by yourself. Wait for me and we'll go to McDonald's after we finish with this box okay?"

"Yeah…you have a deal, Alex," Carly said excitedly.

"Okay, let me take this call and we'll be on our way."

"'Kay," Carly said as she walked toward the kitchen.

"Hello, Mother," Alex said into the telephone.

"Alexandra, what are you doing?"

Alex raised her eyes up toward the ceiling.

"What are you talking about, Mother?"

"Who was that child that called herself your daughter?"

Alex looked toward the kitchen then turned back with a smile on her face. "My daughter, Mother. She is Reese's child."

"Alexandra, your father and I would like to take the opportunity to speak with you during our visit on Thanksgiving."

"I would like that. You can meet Reese and Carly. You're going to like them, Mother and—"

"Alexandra, I don't want to meet with anyone but you," Vanessa said quickly. The silence grew between them.

Alex stood rooted to floor.

"That's why I called. I wanted to ask you not to bring them to Kate's for Thanksgiving. It's only for family, Alexandra. We can talk afterward and resolve all this."

Alex stood in shocked silence. Alex had the feeling that her mother thought she had scored and just shook her head in disbelief before answering. "Did you think this would work?"

"What?"

"How dare you say those things to me?"

"Alexandra…"

"This is something you either accept or you don't. I have nothing to discuss with you. I am taking my family to Kate and Rob's home because we have been invited. If you find that unacceptable, perhaps you should not come, Mother."

"Alexandra, what has gotten into you?"

"I won't have anyone, not even you, tell me who to love. You don't have to like it and you don't have to accept it. But know that this is my life and if you want to remain in my life then perhaps you should think about what you will be saying to me next."

Vanessa was stunned. She suddenly realized that her daughter had tapped into something that she had never really seen. Alexandra stood alone and was strong enough to do so. Vanessa decided that retreat for now was better than an all-out war.

"Alexandra, you are too excited. Perhaps we should discuss this at a later time," Vanessa said politely.

"You don't get it do you? My life is not open for discussion. I choose, not you. Now, I have to go. My daughter is waiting for me to take her to McDonald's. It's too bad, Mother; if you had given them half a chance you would have loved them." Alex hung up the telephone and never looked back.

†

"I spoke to the realtor today. All the bank paperwork is taken care of. We have an offer on your house and she thinks she has a couple who might be interested in this one. Alex?" Reese waited for Alex to respond. Alex, apparently oblivious to the conversation and lost in her thoughts, stood by the window. "Alex?"

"What? I'm sorry, love. What did you say?" Alex asked as she turned to face Reese.

"I was telling you that we can put an offer on that house we both liked."

"That's great," Alex said as she walked over and took Reese in her arms.

"Hey? Are you okay?"

"It's been a difficult last few days. But, yes, I'm fine," Alex said with a smile.

"Alex, you would tell me if something happened right?"

Alex released Reese and took a few steps away.

Reese stood behind her, waiting. "Alex? Has something happened? Have you changed your mind about us?"

Alex turned around immediately. "No, no, nothing has changed between us. I love you,

Reese." She took Reese in her arms again to reassure her. "I had a very unpleasant conversation with Elliot yesterday and with my mother today."

"Why didn't you tell me?" Reese asked.

"I was going to."

"Loving me is alienating you from your life, isn't it?"

"Loving you has given me a life," Alex said as she kissed Reese lightly.

"I'm sorry you're having such a hard time, darling."

"I love you, my funny face," Alex said with a smile.

"Alex, I love you." Reese looked into the eyes of the woman she loved.

Alex returned the look and the clouds that had filled her eyes started to dissipate. "Never doubt my love for you, Reese. That is the one thing in this world that will never fail you. I will always be here. Always and forever. You're stuck with me."

"Always and forever is something I can handle." Reese said as her mouth found Alex's to seal the promise.

Alex quickly pulled away. "Hey! We have to get married!"

"What?" Reese was caught off guard.

"I know that it is only symbolic and all that, but I want to marry you," Alex said with all the love she felt inside.

"I would like that too."

"We should plan this out. We can maybe have a reception at the…"

"Alex?"

"Yes, love?"

"Kiss me. We can plan all you want in the morning," Reese said. Alex smiled and kissed the woman in her arms.

Chapter 14

The ringing of the telephone on the nightstand woke Alex. As she tried to for reach it Reese, still asleep, protested her movement by tightening her arms around her. Alex smiled, reached over, and picked up the annoying telephone.

"Hello?"

"Good morning, Alex."

"God, what is it with you and waking me up? Don't you have anything better to do every weekend? Go make love to your husband or something," Alex said jokingly.

"Already took care of that," Kate laughed.

"Okay, so you have one over on me."

"I got a call from Mother last night. She will be blessing us with her presence. She called to confirm. I thought you should know. She will probably be calling you."

"I already got the call yesterday."

"Everything okay?" Kate asked, the concern showing in her voice.

"No, it's not, Kate. We had a very definite disagreement. We both took a corner, if you know what I mean."

"I'm sorry, Alex, I'll talk to her."

"No, you better not. Some things just have to work themselves out...or not. I remembered what you said, sis, and I fought for my happiness."

"Good for you, Alex. Good for you." Kate's voice showed the smile that she displayed.

"Hey! I'm getting married," Alex said excitedly.

"You're what?"

"You know, married? As in forever and ever?" Alex laughed. "When Reese wakes up and we've all had breakfast, we'll come over and make plans okay?"

"Sounds great. I'll prepare lunch for all of us. And, Alex..."

"Yeah?"

"You did good, sis."

"Thanks, Kate. Thanks." Alex hung up the phone and found Reese looking at her.

"Good morning," Reese said with a dreamy smile.

"Good morning," Alex replied, holding her tighter.

"Alex?"

"Yes, love?"

"I need you."

Alex smiled.

†

Alex was about to knock on Kate's door when it swung open and Kate pulled them all inside excitedly.

"Okay, start to spill," Kate said excitedly.

"Hello to you too," Alex said with a big grin on her face.

"Where is Kevin?" Carly asked immediately.

"He is on the jungle gym, honey, why don't you go out and play with him."

"A jungle gym?" asked Alex.

"Rob's new project."

Reese smiled. Rob was always on a new project. Reese really liked him. He was always one surprise after another. And as much as Kate would get exasperated every time he 'took on another project,' as she put it, you couldn't fail to see the look of love in her eyes every time she said his name.

"Does he ever get tired of new projects?" Alex teased.

The two sisters were now going at it.

Reese rolled her eyes in faked exasperation.

"I'm going to the kitchen for coffee," Reese said and left them both standing there.

Alex and Kate looked at each other and started to laugh at the same time as they followed Reese to the kitchen.

"Okay, so spill," said Kate again when all three were in the kitchen.

Very proud of herself, Alex stated, "We are getting married."

"I got that part, genius," mocked Kate.

"We haven't really made any plans yet," Reese said, then looked adoringly to Alex whose face looked just as goofy.

"Okay, okay you two. Lovey-dovey eyes later; details now," Kate insisted. "How is this going to happen? Details please!"

Reese and Alex smiled at one another and all three women started throwing out ideas.

†

"Hello, Uncle Rob."

"Uncle Rob? I kind of like the sound of that," Rob said with a smile as he opened his arms for the little girl.

He was rewarded with a smile and a kiss. "Thank you," Rob said before releasing her.

"Yeah, you're my uncle now. Alex said that since I am her daughter now that you are my *Uncle Rob*."

Rob smiled.

"Hi," Carly said to a very upset-looking Kevin.

"What does it mean? Are you supposed to be my cousin now?" asked Kevin.

"Yep, we're cousins."

Kevin took off running inside the house.

Rob looked on in surprise.

Carly looked rejected.

Rob turned the little girl to face him. "Hey, Kevin is just confused. You know he thinks you are the cat's meow right?" Rob tried to console the child whose eyes were filling with tears.

†

Kevin ran through the kitchen as the three women looked up. "Hey, no running in the house!" exclaimed Kate. "Kevin?" Kate got up and followed him.

Reese and Alex looked at each other before they both were drawn to the kitchen door again.

Rob was walking in with an obviously upset Carly in tow.

"What happened?" Reese asked concerned as she went to kneel in front of her daughter. Alex looked up and Rob signaled her out of the kitchen.

Alex and Rob left Carly and Reese in the kitchen and walked into the living room

"What happened?" a concerned Alex asked.

"Carly called me *Uncle Rob*, and Kevin got all upset and ran off."

"Why? I thought they got along great. They love playing together." Alex could not figure out what was happening.

"Where is Kate?"

"She went after Kevin," Alex said, distracted. "I better see how things are in the kitchen."

Alex walked into the kitchen to a still crying child.

Reese was sitting in a chair with Carly on her lap, rocking her back and forth. "Honey, I'm sure he still likes you. He must have been upset about something else." Reese tried to comfort her daughter.

Alex just stood there not understanding what had just happened.

†

"Kevin?" Kate called as she entered her son's room. "Hey, what's wrong, sweetheart?"

Kevin stood silently looking out the window.

Kate walked up to him, pulled a chair over next to him, and sat down. "Want to tell me what's wrong?"

"Nothing is wrong. I just wanted to be by myself," he said seriously.

"Ahh…I see." Kate tried another approach. "Wouldn't you rather play outside?"

"No, I want to be up here," he answered, looking down at his hands.

"Did you get upset with Daddy?"

"No."

"Why are you so moody?"

"I'm not moody. I just want to be in my room."

Kate knew she was going nowhere fast. Kevin was so much like his aunt sometimes that she figured that was how she understood his withdrawals sometimes. "Kevin, honey, why don't you just tell me what's wrong and maybe I can help you."

Kevin looked at her with eyes full of questions. He chose to remain silent as he looked out the window again.

Kate waited patiently as so many emotions crossed his face.

Finally, he looked at her. "Is Carly my cousin now?" Kevin asked.

A relieved Kate said, "Yes, honey. Aunt Alex and Reese are going to be a family. So yes, she is your family now too." Kate smiled.

"I don't want her to be my cousin," stated Kevin.

Kate had not expected this. "Kevin, I thought you liked Carly."

Kevin looked away. "I don't want her to be my cousin," he repeated.

"Why? You like her don't you? She is the sweetest little thing." Kate could not believe or understand why her son was reacting this way.

"I don't want her to be my cousin!" he yelled as he ran out of the room.

"Kevin, Kevin!" Kate went after him.

Kevin ran past Rob and out the front door.

Alex walked into the living room and met Rob's and Kate's puzzled eyes. "What's happened?" Alex asked.

"Kevin is very upset and I don't understand why. He just ran out the door," Kate explained as she followed after her son. Rob and Alex stood confused. It seemed that all had fallen apart from one minute to another.

✝

Kate walked back in a few minutes later. "I can't find him, Rob, I'm worried."

Rob went over and took Kate into his arms. "I'll go out and look for him. You just relax. I will find him, don't worry." He kissed Kate and went after Kevin.

"I don't know what happened," Kate said as she sat down. "Where are Reese and Carly?"

"Still in the kitchen. Carly won't stop crying either. She's really upset. I thought they got along really well. Do you think it's because of me, Kate?" Alex's face held the pain she tried to control.

"You? Why you?"

"You know, about my being gay and living with Reese. You think maybe that upset him?" Finally, what she feared was out.

"No, Alex, I don't think it was that," Kate said, trying to reassure her.

"Then why? He likes Reese and he loves Carly. That's the only reason I could think of…he must hate me, Kate." Alex sounded really upset.

"Alex, Kevin loves you. He thinks you are the greatest aunt…and, Alex you are. You have spent time with him and he knows you love him. He is more like you than me. God knows he is just as moody," Kate finished saying in faked exasperation.

"I love the little monster," Alex said with a smile as tears rolled down her face.

"Alex, it's not what you think. We will figure this out."

†

Rob finally found Kevin at the park playground sitting on a swing, dragging his feet in the dirt.

"Hey there, sport. You left the womenfolk back there really worried," Rob said and sat in the swing next to his son.

Kevin just sat looking at the ground. Rob sat next to him for a while before he tried talking to him.

250

"Want to tell me what's really bothering you?"

Kevin looked up at his father. He wanted to tell him but just couldn't. "No." Kevin said softly as his foot started playing with the dirt again.

"You know, sometimes the only way to feel better is by talking to someone you trust."

They continued to sit in silence then suddenly Kevin said, "I don't want Carly to be my cousin."

"Why?" Rob asked.

"I just don't want it," Kevin answered, still looking at the ground.

"You know it wouldn't change anything if she became your cousin. That would mean that she would always be around. And I know you like playing together." Rob tried another approach not understanding why his son was being so stubborn on this issue.

Kevin looked up and met his eyes with a challenge. "It would change everything!"

"No, Kevin, it wouldn't." Rob tried to reassure him.

"I don't want to be her cousin," Kevin repeated again. "I don't want to be her cousin."

"Then what would you like her to be?" Rob asked in controlled frustration.

Kevin looked at his father again and then back at the ground.

Suddenly, Rob understood what the problem was. He sat awhile longer in silence then tried talking to his son again. "You like her a lot don't you?" Rob asked sympathetically.

Kevin didn't answer. "Yeah sure, she's okay," Kevin finally said casually.

BINGO! thought Rob. "You know Uncle Tom married his cousin," Rob mentioned just as casually.

Kevin looked up right away. "Really?" Then he looked down at the dirt again.

"Yeah," Rob answered, looking up at the sky.

"I thought cousins weren't suppose to do that." Kevin was finally talking.

"Well, they weren't really cousins. I mean they were cousins but by marriage. It's okay to marry if you are cousins by marriage, you know." Rob kept acting as if it were just a regular conversation then finally looked down at his son.

Kevin was lost in his own thoughts.

"You think maybe we should go back and finish building that jungle gym?" Rob asked.

Kevin looked up with a smile. "Yeah, Mom wants it finished today." Kevin got up and started walking.

Rob smiled and shook his head as he followed his son home.

†

Kevin walked into the living room past Kate and Alex and went into the kitchen. He stopped in front of Reese, who was still holding Carly.

"Want to go play?" Kevin asked Carly.

"You're not mad at me?" Carly asked sullenly.

"No," he answered looking ashamed. "It's guy stuff. I'm okay now. Come on." He reached out for her and she followed him out the kitchen door holding hands with a smile on her face.

Reese just sat amazed.

From the door, Alex and Kate stood staring as Rob walked past them and went to the refrigerator to get a soda. All three women stared at him.

"You know, it's just guy stuff," he said as he walked out the kitchen door. Three women were left baffled and relieved.

Chapter 15

"Alex! Why are you still there?" Reese asked.

"Reese, honey, something came up at the last minute," Alex said into the telephone. "I am just finishing up, and I'll meet you there. Okay, sweetheart?"

"Okay, I'll call Joanne and tell her we will be running about thirty minutes late to see the house again. And, Alex…"

"Yes, love?"

"I…I'm really nervous. I'm sorry I yelled at you."

Reese sounded out of sorts to Alex. "It's okay, why are you so nervous, love?" Alex sounded concerned now, the papers in front of her forgotten.

"This is a big step, Alex. I…I love you." Reese began to cry.

"Reese, you're crying!" Alex started getting up.

"Alex…"

"What's wrong, Reese? I'm coming home." Alex hung up and ran out the door.

Fifteen minutes later, Alex walked in through the door and found Reese huddled on the far corner of the sofa. Alex walked up to her slowly. She sat down gently and Reese went straight into her arms. She caressed Reese's hair gently and held her fiercely to her. "What's wrong, baby?" Alex asked softly into Reese's hair.

"Alex, I would never hurt you," said Reese.

"I know that, darling. What's got you so upset?"

"Maybe we should wait before we get married," Reese said. The silence was palpable.

"You've changed your mind?" Alex's voice sounded hollow. She could feel Reese's body tense up.

"I think that maybe we should take some time before we take this big step," Reese answered.

"Reese, is this what *you* want?" Alex thought her heart would break.

"I think we have really rushed this and perhaps we should give this relationship a while. If it endures then maybe we should consider it further…"

Before Reese finished Alex released her and got up.

Reese could not tell what Alex's reaction was. All she noticed was Alex's shoulders straightened.

"I think that's a good idea, Reese. I'll call Joanne to cancel. I'll call you later." Alex ran out the door.

†

"Kate, is Alex there?" Reese asked.

Kate was silent on the other side of the telephone. "What's wrong, Reese?"

"I haven't seen her since yesterday. We had words…" Reese broke down.

"Reese, it will be fine. What happened?" Kate was worried. It wasn't like Alex to just run off and not tell her.

"It's complicated, Kate. I think I made a mistake." Reese wasn't making any sense.

"Reese, what happened?"

"Kate, I was so confused. I love her, Kate. I love her…" Reese started crying.

"Oh, shit."

Something inside Kate told her that she had to find Alex. It all felt so wrong and yet so familiar. Memories of what had happened to Alex after Teddy's death flooded her mind, causing her anxiety to rise dramatically. She was almost hysterical with worrying that her sister had hurt herself and she would lose her again. Alex had finally come back from the terrible loss of her son, had finally allowed herself to feel again, to take a chance on life and to allow love to fill not only her body but her very soul. Kate looked down at her hands and noticed they were trembling. She kept staring at her hands when suddenly a horrific thought filled her mind and she bolted into action.

"Oh God, God no," Kate said as she ran to her car.

†

Kate drove through the iron gates of Deslend Cemetery. Kate felt her chest tighten the closer she got to her destination. The cemetery looked empty and cold, the trees bare and barren, the stones of the graves looking forlorn and desolate. Nothing moved, nothing even appeared to be alive as fall claimed nature, pulling it toward the deathly sleep of winter.

"Oh, God, please let her be okay, please," Kate kept repeating as she scanned the graveyard, her eyes searching for just a hint of color among the white and gray. Not even the leaves held any of their former color as they lay on the ground, adding to the sense of abandoned death.

Kate pulled over and looked toward the big white stone of an angel, a statue she had helped pick out. She got out of the car, heading toward the statue. As she got closer she spotted a black coat on the ground near the statue and immediately recognized the coat as Alex's. Her eyes focused on a gray mound amongst the fallen leaves, and she ran. Kate stopped and stared at Alex's body lying on top of Teddy's grave. She fell to her knees.

"Alexandra, get up!" Kate yelled not daring to touch her. Alex did not stir. "Oh, God, Alex, don't do this to me. Please, Alex, please get up!" She cried. She didn't think she could bear this, especially after she had just gotten Alex back. Alex stirred and got up on her knees, her skirt and blouse wrinkled and dirty. Her eyes expressionless. Kate barreled into her, wrapping her arms around her sister, feeling the cold of her body against her. "Alex, oh, Alex!" Kate held on tightly as the cried into her sister's hair.

Alex said nothing as she fell into Kate's embrace. Kate held her tightly. "It's okay, Alex. We are going to make it, okay. Nothing we can't fix together, remember?" Kate kept talking as she stroked Alex's hair. "Reese is worried about you, you know. She called me crying."

"She doesn't want me, Kate." Alex's voice was rough and low. "I'm so tired, Kate. I'm just so tired," she finished in a whisper.

Alex's hand opened and out spilled white pills. Kate looked horrified. She pulled Alex away from her and stared into her eyes. A new fear took over her heart. "Alex! Alex did you take some?" Kate was hysterical now. "Alex, look at me!"

Alex looked at Kate in confusion then down at her hand.

"No."

Kate pulled her back into her embrace. Both sat hanging on to one another on Teddy's grave. Kate held Alex tightly like a child as she rocked back and forth.

†

Kate walked into the house holding Alex. As soon as they walked into Kate's living room, they came face-to-face with Vanessa Masters.

"Mother!" Kate said in surprise. Alex said nothing.

Vanessa took at step forward looking at Alex and the state she was in.

"Alexandra?" Vanessa looked from Alex to Kate. "What's happened?" demanded Vanessa.

"She's upset," Kate said not giving other details. Kate helped Alex sit on the couch. Vanessa sat next to Alex.

"Alexandra, it will pass," Vanessa said softly as her hand reached for her daughter's.

Alex said nothing.

Vanessa looked up at Kate.

"I found her on Teddy's grave," Kate said as her eyes started filling with tears again. Kate turned around but not before Vanessa noticed the tears. "She hasn't said a word since."

"Alexandra, it will pass. In time, you will come to accept it, dear. This is for the best," Vanessa said, trying to console her daughter.

Something struck a chord and Alexandra's eyes went to her mother.

Vanessa smiled and stroked her daughter's hand.

"You talked to her didn't you?" Alex said accusingly.

Kate swirled around with surprise written on her face.

Vanessa just stared at Alex. "Alexandra, I don't know what…" Vanessa started to say.

"You talked to her. How could you have gone so far?" Alex continued.

Kate just stared in disbelief.

Vanessa got up and folded her arms in front of her.

"Mother! You didn't!" Kate said in horror.

"Yes, I did!" Vanessa replied sternly. "Alex's career would be destroyed. She is so confused she doesn't know what she is doing." Vanessa said, defending herself.

"You did this to me?" Alex got up and tears filled her eyes. "You didn't do it for me. You did it for you! It doesn't matter to you that I love Reese and that she makes me happy. You only thought of you!"

"Alexandra, you are not yourself," Vanessa tried to explain.

"I will never, ever will forgive you for this!" Alex said to Vanessa as she ran out the door.

"Alexandra! Come back here!" Vanessa demanded.

As the door closed behind Alex Vanessa was faced with Kate.

"What have you done, Mother?" Kate was furious.

"I did what no one else would do for her. I tried to save her from this depravity. It's not natural, Katherine," Vanessa said in disgust.

"It's not natural? What is natural to you, Mother? You would rather see your child dead than with a woman wouldn't you?" Kate said accusingly.

Vanessa stared in shock.

"Leave my house, Mother. Leave right now!"

Vanessa stared in disbelief.

Kate stood her ground.

Vanessa turned around, picked up her purse, and walked out.

†

Alex ran into the house looking for Reese.

Kate had already called and Reese, upon hearing Alex, ran down the stairs and into her arms.

Both hung on to each other tightly.

"I love you. I love you, Alex. I love you," Reese kept saying.

"I love you too, baby. I love you too." Alex held Reese tightly.

"Alex, I'm sorry…Kate told me she found you," said Reese as she looked at Alex hand and caressed Alex's hair. "I'm sorry Alex. I…"

"I know why," said Alex as she looked at Reese with tear-filled eyes.

Reese took her into her arms again, kissing her repeatedly then gently pulling out of her arms and leading her upstairs to their room.

"Come, come, my love." Reese helped her take her clothes off and after she removed her own clothing, she got under the sheet with Alex. "I love you, Alex."

The tears ran down Alex's face and Reese started kissing them away. "I promise nothing will come between us again." Her kisses were soft and soothing.

Their lovemaking that afternoon sealed their relationship forever. The kisses were soft and the caresses were slow. When they both came, they held on to each other with the understanding that they would never let go of one another ever again.

Chapter 16

"Well, I have to admit the house is gorgeous, Reese," Rose said as she looked around.

"Carly fell in love with the pool. And that is all that Alex needed to hear. That child has her wrapped around her little finger," Reese said, smiling.

"Yep, it's a beautiful place. Now all you need is furniture."

"That…yeah."

"What?"

"Won't you please sit down, Rose?" Reese gestured flamboyantly to the floor.

Rose started laughing and sat down on the floor.

"Well, in the end we decided to start fresh. We put most of the furniture in consignment and the rest we just donated to the Salvation Army."

"Starting from scratch, huh?"

"New life in every aspect of the word." Reese's face had a big smile.

"Well, the house is huge. Have you started shopping for furniture yet?" Rose said.

"Alex has been really busy with a case lately…" Reese's smile dulled a little.

"Anything wrong?"

"I think she is having a hard time with one of her colleagues." Reese looked down at her hands as she spoke.

"Have you asked her about it?"

"Alex, is processing…it drives me crazy but that is just the way she deals. I have learned to see the signs. We have argued endlessly about it. She has had a hard time, Rose. I just don't want to push right now."

Rose put her hand over her friend's. "The mother did a job on her didn't she?"

"Yeah, she really did. Alex has been through hell. And I didn't help any," Reese said sadly.

"Don't blame yourself, Reese. That woman goes beyond anything I have ever seen. She used your love for Alex to persuade you. You are totally without blame," insisted Rose.

"I didn't have to listen, Rose, I should have used better judgment."

"Honey, hindsight is something we all wish for," Rose said sadly.

"You didn't see her that day, Rose. In some ways she hasn't been the same since," Reese said sadly.

"Reese, Alex worships you. Don't go putting any ideas in your head. What happened was not your fault. It is that woman that is to blame. You two love each other. Don't let anything stop you from enjoying your good fortune. Because, Reese, if you allow it, she wins."

Reese hugged her friend. "I love you, Rose, You are a good friend."

"Ahem!" Both women turned simultaneously at the sound.

"What are you doing with my future wife?" asked Alex with her hands on her hips.

Reese and Rose stared at one another and then back at Alex.

Alex couldn't hold it anymore and started laughing.

Reese jumped up and went into Alex's arms.

Rose got up, dusting off her pants.

"Hello, beautiful," Alex said as she looked at Reese.

"Hello, gorgeous."

"How was your day?"

"Slaved away, cleaning all this furniture!"

Alex looked around critically then nodded. "You did a good job, the place looks great."

"Okay, you two," interrupted Rose, "When are you going furniture shopping?"

Alex and Reese looked at each other and then at Rose. "Tomorrow," they said at the same time and then started to kiss.

Rose shook her head in jest. "They just have to work on the everyday details," she said to herself.

✝

"Kate, I told you I hate that color!" Alex said for the fourth time.

"But, Alex, mauve is very fashionable."

"It's pink…I hate pink, Kate!"

"Okay, then what color do you suggest?"

"I don't know. Whatever Reese picks is fine, I guess."

"That's what she says. You are both going to kill me, you know that right?"

Alex started laughing. "Okay, okay, let's look at the colors again."

"How about this blue one then?"

"Umm…no, it's too drippy," said Alex, looking at the swatch in front of her.

"Drippy! Drippy? What is drippy?" Kate said in exasperation. "Reese said you would decide. Now decide! You are getting married in two weeks and I need to order this dress. "Pick a color or die!"

"All right…all right," Alex said, looking at the book again. The phone rang and Kate picked up.

"Hello?"

"Hi, Kate."

"Reese, she still hasn't picked the color!" Kate complained, and Alex stuck her tongue out at her.

"Let me talk to her, Kate."

"All right, see if you can reason with her. If you don't you may have a casualty on your hands by the time you get back. I swear, she is driving me crazy!" Kate finished saying before handing the phone to Alex.

"Hello, sweetheart," Alex said with a big smile on her face.

"Hello, darling. Giving Kate a hard time?"

"Me?"

"Yes, you!" Reese laughed. "Put her out of her misery, darling. Will you do that?" Reese played along.

"Since you have asked me…yes." Alex let out a loud laugh. "When will you be back?"

"Day after tomorrow. Momma is much better."

"I'm sorry I couldn't go with you, Reese, I really feel awful about that."

"I understand, Alex. This case is very important to you. You concentrate on that case so we can have an uninterrupted honeymoon. Everything is okay here."

"Did you tell them?" Alex asked with concern.

"Yes."

"And?"

"I love you, Alex, that is all that matters to me," Reese said with a sad note in her voice.

"I'm sorry, sweetheart."

"Yes, I am too."

"I love you. Come home, Reese, or I will come and get you." Alex started getting agitated.

"Alex…"

"Please?"

"Darling, nothing is going to come between us, I promise you. I love you, Alex. I love you more than life itself. Now pick the color of your sister's dress so we can get one step closer to our wedding okay?"

"'Kay, I love you, Reese."

"I love you, too, darling. Remember that…always remember that."

"Okay, bye, sweetheart. I'll talk to you to-night."

"Goodbye, darling."

Alex hung up the phone and looked at Kate. "Okay, slave driver." She picked up the swatches and pointed to one.

"That's pink! You said you hated pink!" Kate said in frustration.

"It's not pink, it's coral."

"Alex, you are going to kill me. You are going to kill me!"

Chapter 17

Alex woke up with a kiss. Her eyes fluttered open and she stared into the bluest eyes she had ever seen and smiled.

"Hello, lover."

"How did you…?"

"I took the last flight out…I missed you." And after saying that, she kissed Alex again.

"Welcome home."

†

"Alex, stop pacing!"

"I am not pacing, Kate!"

"Okay, if you don't stop walking from one side of the room to another I am going to be sick!"

"Do you think maybe something happened?"

"No, nothing happened. It's still early. Now relax!"

"But, Katie…"

"Oh no! Don't *but Katie* me. I have had at least three heart attacks with you and you almost gave me an ulcer with the dress thing. Now sit!"

"All right," said Alex as she pouted.

They heard a car pull up and both ran to the window.

"She's here!" Alex said in both excitement and relief.

Kate looked at Alex and smiled. "Now let's go. And remember, Alex, just let yourself be happy."

"Kate…" Alex said as her eyes began to fill with unshed tears.

"I know…I know."

Both sisters held each other. "Now, let's go and get you married."

†

The church was filled with flowers and as the music began all eyes turned to the rear. Slowly, the guests' faces filled with smiles as they saw Carly walk in wearing a beautiful white lacey dress with a creamy coral-colored sash around her waist. She dropped petals out of a basket onto the floor as she walked down the aisle. Kevin was walking beside her in a black tux, holding a small cushion with the rings that Alex and Reese would give each other. Next Kate walked in wearing a soft, gauze coral dress. She walked slowly and happily in the knowledge that she had finally gotten Alex this far.

Alex will finally be happy, thought Kate and that made her smile even brighter.

When both children reached the altar and Kate stood next to them, Rose walked down the aisle and stood next to Kate smiling as well. The music once again announced a new arrival.

Alex was a vision of beauty as she walked down the aisle. Happiness poured out of her. She walked slowly with a new sense of purpose. She would make this relationship work. Finally, Reese would be forever hers. Alex looked at Carly as she approached the altar and gave her a big smile. Carly smiled at Kevin and Kevin pulled at his collar.

Alex reached the altar, kissed Kate, and winked at Rose who smiled in return.

Then, once again, the music started and Reese stood at the entry to the sanctuary. Both women looked at one another in awe. They had agreed not to see each other's dress before the wedding. Now, Reese just stood looking at Alex and Alex's eyes captured Reese. Each was thinking how beautiful the other looked. As the music cued again, Reese started walking to her love.

They faced each other as the minister said the words. Beautiful words that neither heard. All that filled their ears was the beating of their hearts. The minister touched Alex's arm and nodded. This was the signal for her to speak. Alex took Reese's hand in hers and placed the ring on her finger.

"Reese, I love you. I never thought I would feel love again. In finding you, I found all the beauty that I thought was lost to me. In finding you, I found that which makes me whole. In finding you, I found not only love but also hope. In finding you. I found a child; a child that we will love and share and raise together. I love you, Reese. I love you with all that I am."

Reese smiled as a tear ran down her cheek. Then Reese took Alex's hand and placed the ring on her finger. She took a deep breath and looked into the eyes of the woman she loved.

"Alex, you are such a gift to me. I only dreamed of love. I wished to the heavens and my gift was you. You are such a beautiful soul, Alex. You have shown me that tenderness exists and that love endures. You have shown me that there is no limit to loving. I want to spend the rest of my life loving you. I promise to share your days and your nights. I promise to help make your dreams come true. I promise to give you all the joy that is in my power. I promise to be yours forever till the end of time."

Alex squeezed Reese's hand.

"I love you," Alex said softly as a tear escaped her eye as well.

Then the minister said the words, "You are now one," and with those words, lips met and two hearts now beat as one.

The world stood still and the only two people that existed among the fog were two lovers.

"You are so beautiful, Alex."

"You are the beautiful one. If you only knew."
"Knew what, darling?"
"What makes me happy."
"What makes you happy, darling?"
"The very thought of you…the very thought of you, my love."

About the Author

S. Anne Gardner

S. Anne Gardner has lived all over the world and is now living on the East Coast of the United States. She has a love that fills her heart and children who fill her life. She has many interests and is a published author as well as a published poet. She enjoys sailing, horseback riding, art, traveling, reading, and writing. Her family, her friends, and her music fill her life in a world that is her own.

E-Books, Print, Free e-books

Visit our website for more publications available
online.

www.affinityebooks.com

Published by Affinity E-Book Press NZ Ltd
Canterbury, New Zealand
Registered Company 2517228